The Hatchet Killer

Written by:

Brandon Adkins

Contents

Chapter One:

Spring break, the perfect time of the year. Finally, the winter has come to an end, midterms are done, and we have a couple of weeks to be free. I've been waiting for spring break of my junior year of college ever since I started here at Prescott University. My best friend and I have been waiting to finally get out of the state and have our girls all alone at last. Some might think that we're going to party but not for us. Most kids are going south towards beaches and wild places for spring break. John and I decided to go to West Virginia for our break. You may ask us why WV instead of Florida or California, but the answer is simple: isolation, wilderness, and my parents own a log cabin on the outskirts of Elkins.

Elkins is a small town in West Virginia. The scenery there is remarkable. No matter where you looked, you saw beautiful landmarks of forest-covered mountains. It was perfect for isolation, with the feeling of being surrounded by nature's greatness. The temperatures range from the 50s to the 60s, the perfect temps. It's neither too hot nor too cold, nothing overbearing or underwhelming. The nights get quite chilly, but nothing a nice fire couldn't handle.

My dad had a log cabin that was built by his father in the early 1900s. The cabin was a little past Elkins near Spruce. Spruce was a ghost town by this point in time due to the coal mining company that moved to Luke, Maryland. My father now travels there for his business; since then he had moved up the ladder where he doesn't have to be at the mine all the time. The cabin was built near Shavers Fork, a river that runs into Spruce Knob Lake.

The area surrounding the river is covered in forest and rock. With Spruce being a ghost town and having the cabin surrounded by forest and water, it was perfect for complete isolation, the way I liked it. My father was finally fine with me using the cabin for a few weeks, because he knew I was only using it with my best friend and our companions.

Julie, my girlfriend, was very happy when I brought this plan up to her our freshman year at Prescott. We dated for a few months before I came up with the plan, but I knew she'd love the idea. She's the type of girl that loves the woods, loves getting dirty and being adventurous. She's simply amazing, always wearing a cowgirl hat outside of school since she's originally from Texas and always wearing boots and flannels. She always caught my eye, which I loved. She was almost my height with blonde hair and blue eyes. Her personality was simply amazing, always smiling and always energetic. She was very smart and took her schoolwork extremely seriously but at the same time knew how to have a good time. So, she wasn't a drag to be around, making her traits proportional.

John came into my dorm just in time. Always in a rush that guy is. He's built, like me, part of Prescott's baseball team. He's the pitcher, so he's like the quarterback on a football team. Always getting the spotlight and the fame. Surprisingly, he had the smarts, but at the same time he was quite gullible and dumb-minded. He either knew how to find trouble or trouble seemed to find him. His attitude towards life was stern and lively.

I'm also on the baseball team along with him as the designated hitter. Don't get me wrong; I get some fame too for getting most of the hits on our team but not as much as pretty boy does. We both get a lot of attention from other students and teachers. I look at myself as the muscle and see him as the architect on the team.

"Are you ready yet? What's taking you forever we still need to go get the girls." He said.

"I'm just about done packing. You know I've been waiting for this day to come for a couple years. I just want it to be perfect."

"It'll be fine; you always overthink things."

"I do not!"

"No time to argue; just hurry up," He said impatiently.

I grab my bag and my keys and turned the light off. I hurry down the stairs with John towards my car. She's my pride and joy. I've always loved driving around in it. The car was my graduating gift from my dad. She's a 1954 Pontiac Star Chief convertible equipped with a straight-eight engine, Hydramatic transmission, and power steering and brakes. Those are only some of the features, including its cherry red body paint with its cream-colored leather seats. My father found and bought it from a junkyard out in West Virginia on his way home from the cabin on the last visit he had there. My father took the car to my uncle, who fixed her up. If anything happened to my car, I would feel like I've lost something very special to me. I couldn't imagine life without that car or even see myself in any other car.

I started the car up, listening to the lovely purr coming from her engine. We turned up the music; the sound of *Good Vibrations* by the Beach Boys began to blare out of the speakers as we headed to Molly's house. By the time we reached the house, we noticed the girls had their stuff on the ground next to them. Of course, Julie looked amazing as always with her bright white smile. She had on a pair of brown boots, tight jeans, a pink flannel and her brown cowgirl hat.

She never goes anywhere without that hat; it's her prize possession, making her feel at home. Molly, John's girlfriend, was almost similar to Julie except she's shorter with blonde hair and had on a low-cut shirt with tight jeans, highlighting her perky tits and toned ass. She was smoking hot, but not exactly my type. My father always told me to watch out for a 10; those hard bodies are nothing but trouble.

Julie sat behind me and Molly sat behind John. When Julie got into the car, she gave me a kiss, and I kissed her back, taking in her gorgeous smile and soft lips. Molly gave John a kiss as well, seeing him smirk excitedly. I looked around to see if everyone was ready and drove away. The weather was beautiful out, not too hot, not too cold, and perfect for a car ride. The sun was out, shining down on the girls in the back seat, making Julie's smile even brighter and making Molly's hair glow astonishingly. The sun gave off a ray of warm air, battling the cool breeze from the shield of the few clouds in the atmosphere. The sky was a beautiful blue, making the day even better than what it already was.

"We have to make sure we have plenty of gas." I said as I looked at my fuel gauge. My tank was about half full, but I always get anxious from the thought of running out of gas, especially going on a trip. I've always preferred a full tank as often as possible. I've never let my tank get below half a tank; call me crazy but I like to be prepared for anything.

"And plenty of beer too." John said immediately after me.

"I second that!" I smiled at the fact that our concerns are polar opposites. I'd hate to run out of gas and John would hate to run out of alcohol, as gas would be a second priority in his book.

"Wait, what about wine?" Julie exclaimed.

"We'll stop at the gas station before we head out."

We came up to the gas station by the border before we entered West Virginia. The gas station was run down and looked like no one had been there in a while. The sign was half lit up but still able to make out the words. It read: **Lou's Gas Station**. There was a tow truck off to the side that looked like it hadn't been running in a while. Next to the tow truck there was a beat-up pickup truck that looked like it had been through a lot over the years. Rust ate at the body paint on the undercarriage, and the muffler seemed to be touching the ground. The windows were tinted black, blocking out what I would imagine to be a pile of shit inside the truck. There was a set of lights on top of the roof and half of them were broken.

As I stepped out of my car, I noticed a garage next to the store. The inside was a mess with junk cluttering the entire room. The garage gave off the impression that it hadn't been in operation for many years. The area surrounding the store would have given anyone the chills with its spooky, eerie look to it. Even the fuel pumps looked run-down as the paint was chipped away, rust forming all around. I would be astonished if any gas came out of this thing. With a look of disgust, I headed towards the front door of the store.

The inside of the store looked disgusting, as if no one even bothered with the upkeep. There were spider webs throughout and flies everywhere. The shelves were half stocked and very dusty. The only good thing about the place was the alcohol was well-stocked. There was a constant humming noise coming from the lights hanging above, from the ones that are still working. At the front counter there was a short selection of cigarettes and other miscellaneous items that tempted you to buy more random shit that you don't need. The miscellaneous items were probably all expired anyways based on the look of this shithole.

I headed over to the beer section and grabbed a couple cases of Coors Light and a bottle of wine. As I walked up to the front counter, I asked for a couple packs of Marlboro Reds 100's.

The man behind the counter would have given anyone the creeps. Most of his teeth were missing and with whatever teeth remained, they were all yellow, giving off a frightening smile. He seemed like he was chewing on something constantly, since his mouth moved continuously. Probably a big dip packed into his gums. The man had a very strong odor. The type of odor that would stay in your nostrils for hours. The smell was pretty vile, like a freshly caught cod that sat outside in the dry heat for days. The man had on worn-out greasy-looking overalls. To top things off, the moles on the top of his bald head were the most horrific part about him. They weren't your typical mole spots that one would have on their body. These were covered in tiny hairs and almost a scabby look to them. The area surrounding the moles was red, making it seem like they irritated him, causing him to scratch at them constantly.

"Spring Break, I take it?" The man asked as I set everything on the counter, giving off a smile, or what was considered a smile with his few stained yellow teeth.

"Indeed, it is." I replied.

"Where you headed?"

"Elkins, West Virginia sir. My parents own a cabin just on the outskirts of it."

"You kids be careful out there." He warned as he licked his lips in an odd, creepy way.

"We will be." I answered, not thinking about why he would say that.

"Will that be all for you?"

"No, I'm going to need some gas as well."

"That your car out there?" He asked as he continued to lick his lips, glaring at me awkwardly.

"Yes, sir." I answered respectfully, trying to look away from his creepy stare and trying to ignore his constant lip licks.

"She's a beauty."

"Thank you, sir." I said politely as I started to grow impatient with this gross encounter.

"How much gas?"

"$20 worth."

"Alright, total will be $70.50."

I handed the man a crisp hundred-dollar bill; he took it from my hand with his shaky old hands, punched the total in the register and gave me my change.

"$29.50 is your change."

"Thank you, sir, have a great night."

As I walked out, the old man called back out, "Be careful." The man stared at me on the way out, but he didn't seem like he was exactly staring at me as if through me into some bliss. The way he looked at me gave me a chill down my spine. The man was very odd, and I began to ponder on his warning. I didn't think much of it and put everything in the backseat next to the girls and got into the driver's seat.

"Why's that man just staring at us?" Molly asked, concerned.

"Probably because he's never seen human beings in a long time; just look at this place." John replied sarcastically.

"You have no idea the encounter I just had." I said, ignoring John's sarcasm, as a feeling of relief washed over me as we were about to hit the road again.

I pulled away from the gas station and sped down the road towards Elkins. The drive was beautiful. The scenery was amazing with all the trees and rivers surrounding the place. It was a nice warm night and only had a few more hours to go. I looked in the rearview mirror and noticed both the girls were passed out and John, sitting next to me, was also passed out. Looking at them made me get extremely tired and had a hard time staying awake, so I took a cig out and lit it, turning up the volume a little bit on the radio.

A news station was the only station coming in out here, since we're pretty much in the middle of nowhere now. The man talking was going on and on about the weather. I didn't catch his name, but I did catch that the weather was going to be fair until mid-week, when we were expecting rain. After the weather update the local news came on, and they went on and on about drug busts in the area. Heroin bust here, Meth bust here. I was just glad the girls passed out, because I didn't want them to get sketched out and want to turn back around. I didn't get why people would get into that shit these days. My dad never had these problems out this way growing up or not that he told me anyway.

After the man on the radio was done gossiping about all these drug busts, he got my attention on one thing. A serial killer was on the loose, and his signature move was to cut the heads off his victims. I thought it was just a myth or a campfire story but apparently, bodies were turning up out here with their heads missing. It's a shame to have this bad rep going around when Elkins isn't too far from the last victim and it's supposed to be known for its greatest scenic landscapes.

I yawned and turned the radio off. I was tired of hearing all the bad news and didn't want to think about it at all. I flicked the cig out of my window before the cherry fell out and burned my leather seats. I would've been pissed at myself, probably more pissed than my coach yelling at me for smoking in the first place for being such an important member on the baseball team. I passed by a sign that said, "Elkins: two miles," and woke up real fast since we were close to my cabin.

I had to go through Elkins a little bit to get closer to Spruce, and off to the side was a road that led me back out to the woods near the city limits to where my private property sign was. The city was quiet at night. There was no one out on the streets making it seem like a ghost town. Elkins is small but not small enough to look like no one lives here. Maybe it's the serial killer that has everyone hiding inside; the thought made me shiver as I finally came close to my driveway.

The last time I was out here, I was a little boy when I was still in grade school. My parents would take me out here on breaks to get away from the real world while my father went to work at the mine. It was so peaceful: lovely people everywhere you went, beautiful scenery, an amazing lake nearby and just quiet. Now coming back, it looked different. The road to the cabin seemed long and eerie. The thought of someone popping out of the woods kept haunting my thoughts, making me hurry even faster to the end of the drive.

I finally pulled up to the cabin and woke everyone up. Everyone stepped out of the car and gave a long stretch. They were all yawning and rubbing their eyes, annoyed they had to be woken up but also relieved that they were finally out of the car. I walked up to the front door and unlocked the door. John unloaded the car and brought everything into the house, while the girls ran off to the rooms. The cabin wasn't a huge place, but it was very roomy for us to all be comfortable for the next couple of weeks. It had three bedrooms, but we only needed two, one for Julie and me and one for John and Molly. There was a bathroom in the hall, along with a bathroom in the third bedroom; that way we didn't have to fight for a bathroom in the morning.

The kitchen was huge, the way mother wanted it; that's the only place she goes to escape. She used to make the best meals when she put her mind to it. Always filled the whole cabin up with all kinds of scents. Whether it was cookies with the sweet, sugary, chocolatey smell or all kinds of spices when she made roasts and chicken. The scent of thyme, garlic, onion, basil, oregano, and parsley illuminated the air.

The living room was spacious, with all leather chairs and couches next to a stone fireplace. Glass windows all over the cabin, the biggest windows I've ever seen. The dining room always caught my eye, with an oak table with a white chandelier dangling above it. Outside the cabin there was a decent-sized backyard with an outdoor fireplace and a deck for the pool. On the side was an area for a hot tub; my father put that out there for him to escape and relax after long hours of work. In the front yard, there was a porch with a swing. Off to the side was a flower bed that contained the most beautiful flowers, creating a peaceful vibe. The cabin was perfect, like one you'd see in the movies.

After everyone was situated in their rooms, they gathered in the living room near the fireplace. John started the fire while everyone else took a seat on the couch. We were all pretty tired as we stared at the fire, getting lost in the orange and yellow glow and listening to the wood speak as it cracks and dances. I was so relaxed to the point where I was dozing off. I got up and announced I was retiring for the night. I walked into the room, which I claimed as mine years ago, and climbed into my bed with my silk sheets, waiting for Julie to come into the room.

After what seemed like forever, Julie finally came into the room. She laid down next to me and smiled.

"I love your smile so much."

"Thank you. I love yours too." She smiled even harder.

"You like the place so far?" I asked hopeful.

"Yes, I love it. It's so cozy." She answered happily.

"Just wait till we go exploring; you'll love it even more. I had this planned for years."

"I know I remember the first time you asked me about this; I was so excited and nervous."

"Nervous?" I asked feeling curious and anxious.

"Yes, because I've never been in the middle of nowhere before."

"We're not in the middle of nowhere though." I give off a slight laugh.

"I know, but it seems so isolated, and I thought I might not have liked it, but it feels so nice, so different and it's nice for a change."

"Well, I'm glad you like it. I wanted you to be happy, and I hope the rest of the time here will be nice, just like I've always had so much fun in the past."

After the last comment, it grew quiet for a long moment as we just looked at each other with awestruck eyes. She laid her head on my chest and was out cold. It took me a little longer to fall asleep, but when I did, I was out.

Chapter Two:

The next morning came way too fast as the sun shone through the bedroom window. The smell of the morning air seeped through with the sound of the birds chirping so beautifully. I looked over, and the bed was empty. The smell of breakfast rushed into my nostrils, and instantly the memories of my mother being in the kitchen making her amazing breakfast flowed through my mind. I got up, slipped on my house shoes and walked towards the kitchen. As I entered the kitchen, Julie and Molly were busy cooking us breakfast. John was sitting down at the table waiting for me to join him.

The smell of bacon and maple syrup filled the house as it mixed with the smell of fresh-brewed coffee. The sound of toast came from the counter as it popped up.

"Cheesy eggs, just the way I like them." I said staring hard with hunger-filled eyes.

"I know you all so well." Julie replied, giving me that beautiful smile she always does.

"Coffee Mike?" Molly asked as I sat down.

"Is that even a question Molly?" I said sarcastically as I'm waiting like a little kid for a piece of candy. Give me the biggest cup we have!

"You got it boss." She replied with even more sarcasm.

As I got the cup, I looked down at the hot liquid and took a long whiff of the strong coffee beans as the steam passed through my nose. The best smell God has ever created. Nothing was better in the morning than that strong, wonderful scent. I looked around the table and noticed a copy of The Elkins News Herald and picked it up.

I first looked at the sports page. It was filled with stories from WVU basketball from the season that was coming to an end and went on to the next article about their baseball team. I always wanted to play for WVU but decided to go to Prescott instead. I flipped the page and moved on to the weather articles. Nothing different from the weatherman on the radio during the drive, so I skimmed through the words, trying to move on to more local news. The next page had articles about the serial killer. In big bold words it read: **The Hatchet Killer Strikes Again**. Instantly I got curious and continued reading as I sipped on the scalding hot coffee. The article read:

I didn't get to finish the article because Julie looked over and saw me nose-deep in the newspaper and I didn't want her to get a hold of the paper, so I threw it out, turned around and smiled at her. It seemed to work because she smiled back and asked me how my breakfast was. I looked up and said that everything was perfect. The eggs were cooked perfectly with the cheese properly proportioned. The bacon wasn't overcooked or too crunchy either. Every bite made my mouth water for another till the plate was completely gone.

"What shall we do today?" John asked.

"How about a nice walk to look at the scenery?" I replied.

They all bobbed their heads in agreement. We all slowly started to get up from the kitchen to prepare for the day ahead of us. I went back to the bedroom and headed towards the bathroom to take a shower. I got the water ready as I prepared myself to take the shower. I needed the water hot. Hot enough to the point where it almost burns your skin, but not hot enough that it actually burns. I stood in the shower and let the water almost massage my muscles. I didn't want to get out; it was so relaxing and refreshing to just stand there. I got out of the shower to dry myself off and turned off the water. I got dressed and moved back to the bedroom. As I entered through the door to the bedroom, Julie was already dressed and ready to go.

We all gathered in the living room and headed out the front door. It was a nice warm morning with the sun shining on us. It was beautiful, not a slither of cold air or the feel of unbearable humid air. It was just right. We walked down my long driveway to head towards the local stores not too far away from the cabin. There was a nice antique store that I used to love checking out when I was a kid and told them about it, so that was first on our list.

As we finally got close to the store, the sign read: **Frank's Famous Antiques**. Frank was a nice old man, the nicest guy one can ever meet. We had many talks when I was growing up about all sorts of things, mostly about how he found most of the shit inside of his store. We walked through the door and looked around. I moved to the front counter where Frank was and politely said hello.

"Mike, is that you?" He asked surprised.

"Yes, sir." I replied in a polite manner.

"How old are you now?"

"21."

"Then knock it off with the sir shit."

"Sorry."

"Call me Frank from now on; we're both adults and you're not holding your mommy's hand anymore."

I looked at him shocked because I had never seen this side of him before. Then again, I was young and always came in with my parents, so I had to use my manners.

"You're looking good kid, lot better than I do. You smoke?"

"I do."

"A habit you shouldn't have picked up. Look at what happened to me." He let out a laugh.

He did look worse than I remembered. He wasn't young, but he didn't look this old either. The last time I saw him, he looked in great health, was very well dressed, and had a full head of hair. Now standing here looking at him, he was starting to go bald, and his cough was terrible. Every other minute seemed like he would cough shit up; it was very unpleasant to be around. He even seemed to not care how he dressed anymore either. His clothes used to be well pressed.

Dressed as if headed to a fashion show. He used to wear button-up collared shirts that were tucked into his dress pants and shiny dress shoes. Looking at him now, his clothes weren't presentable. He had on a dirty flannel shirt with stains all over, untucked from his holey jeans. I couldn't see the shoes on his feet, but I assumed they were raggedy as well. Frank's teeth used to be bright white; now they were stained yellow from the amount of coffee and cigs he pounded on a daily basis.

"You're looking nice as well." I lied trying to keep a straight face.

"Bullshit. No need to lie to me Mike. I know I look like shit, but that's beside the point. What are you kids doing out this way?"

"We're on break and I decided to bring my friends up here to enjoy my parents' cabin and to relax from all the stress we had during our exams. The weather is perfect, and I feel like we're going to have a great time up here."

"I wouldn't say a great time." He said sternly.

"Why you say that?" I asked cautiously.

"Because of all the shit that's been going on around here lately."

"I'm not following. What kind of shit has been going on around here? This was such a quiet, friendly place to be."

"Have you not been current with the news lately kid?"

"I've heard some things and read a few things. So?"

"This killer isn't a joke kid. Bodies have been turning up left and right lately. Why you think people have been staying inside lately and only coming out if they really need to?"

"It can't be that bad. I mean, it's not a laughing matter but come on, you seriously think he's going to kill the whole town? The police will find him in no time and things will soon go back to normal. Not the same, of course but better."

"All I'm saying is, careful till this all blows over kid. It'll be a shame if something happened to one of you young kids." He shot me a warning look.

"I appreciate the warning, but no need to freak me out." I said holding back my worried expression.

"Sorry kid, just trying to look out for you is all."

"Well, do me a favor and don't talk about the killings around my friends. I don't need them to run around here all worked up, ruining a good time."

We both put out our cigarettes at the same time and entered the store. Frank went back behind the counter and I went over to my friends.

"There you are! Where were you?" Julie asked concerned.

"I was catching up with Frank. Haven't seen him in years; it was nice to speak to him again."

"Well, don't go wandering off without letting me know. I was worried."

"I'm sorry I won't anymore, I promise." I said trying not to laugh.

I was trying not to smile, but all I kept thinking about was my mother telling me the exact same thing: to not wander off all the time. I'm a very curious guy and tend to just disappear constantly and cannot help it. We looked around a bit longer at some of the items Frank had in his store.

He had all kinds of stuff, anywhere from antique weapons to posters and pictures to old knickknacks. We went up and down the aisles, looking at pretty much everything in the store. By the time they were done with the last shelf, I was starting to get impatient because I'd seen this stuff a hundred times already and wanted to be outside enjoying the day.

I looked at Frank on our way out and gave him a polite goodbye. He also gave me a goodbye along with a 'be careful' look. Everywhere I went there's always talk about this killer and I was starting to get annoyed by it. I came up here for peace, not to keep hearing about this killer on the loose. I kept thinking about how my friends didn't hear anything about this killer, but at the same time I was glad because that's the last thing I need them to give me shit about.

Chapter Three:

I led everyone towards the woods and exclaimed that the scenic trail was amazing and that they had to see it. My parents used to take me down this trail all the time, and I was always in awe of the way the trees drowned out the noise of people and how beautiful the streams were. Even though most of the trees were lying down half dead and covered in green moss. The trail was covered with pine trees all around, making the only thing you'd be able to see is the trail in front of you or the part of the trail you've already come down.

The streams were beautiful in their own way. They were mainly covered with rocks of all sorts of sizes. The sound of the small current running through the rocks sounded so peaceful. The best part was the lake at the end of the trail where we had lunch several times and caught the most fish when my father and I felt like fishing.

The lake was so beautiful, surrounded by trees and rocks. The trees would go on for miles. You wouldn't be able to see anything else in sight. The base of the lake had a lining of giant rocks. If you stood in the right spot and looked in the water, you could see the trees' reflection. The reflection was pure isolation.

The smell of fresh air that comes along with the cool breeze is a beautiful scent that one cannot ever get tired of. Looking straight up and taking in the air is always refreshing. You can't get that in the city with all the polluted air that people breathe in every day of their lives, missing out on the clean crisp air that is out here. I looked around towards the woods nearby the trail, listening to the birds' chirps and the sound the leaves make from the breeze shaking them around lightly.

We continued down the beautiful trail to the area I used to go for our picnics. It wasn't too far away from the start of the trail but far enough to enjoy the scenery that surrounds us. We walked over to the table off to the side and set up our lunch. The table was worn down over the years from the weather. The table was brown with black circles to prove it was aging. There were markings engraved in the table as well. The markings struck me as weird. I had never remembered seeing them before, but there were slash marks, like someone was tallying up a count for something. Near the tally marks there seemed to be a list of initials in an orderly fashion, all lined up right next to each other. Initials that I don't know but it seemed to me like I've seen them somewhere before but can't remember where. Some of the initials were:

Those were just four initials that were listed; there were at least twenty more of them in the same order.

Closer to the lake, there was a building that looked like a shed but was much bigger, more like a garage. The building was new too. I had never seen it there before and looked like someone just built it recently, a couple years back. Once again, I don't remember seeing it, but for some reason in the back of my mind it looked familiar and I started feeling weird. I can't recall the feeling and I know that I've never seen these objects before, but it seems like I'm having a déjà vu moment.

I looked at all my friends sitting at the table with me and they seemed to be enjoying themselves not wondering or noticing the things that I've been seeing. All I can ask myself is why? Why am I noticing these things instead of having fun with my friends? It seems like they only care about the food they're scarfing down their throats and not looking around, seeing what I see. In that moment noticing that everyone was enjoying their lunch, I looked down and saw that I had barely touched mine.

Julie looked at me and finally noticed I didn't touch my food and asked me what was wrong. I looked up and said I wasn't feeling well and wasn't all that hungry anymore, and all I wanted to do was head back. I sat around waiting for them to be done eating their lunch and continued to pick at my food. My mind was racing a million miles an hour. When they finally finished their food, I helped pack everything up and started walking down the path back to the cabin. This time instead of looking around at the scenery, I couldn't get those names out of my head or the shed- or garage-looking building near the lake.

The images seemed like they were haunting my mind on the walk back. As if I couldn't get rid of them from my thoughts. I kept telling myself that groups of people like ourselves came and had lunch at the same spot and carved their initials into the table, which happens anywhere you go. Then I told myself that someone must have built the building to store stuff for the lake like boats or something. That's not too weird to see by a body of water, so I left it at that and grabbed Julie's hand as we headed down the trail back to the cabin

As we entered the door to the cabin, Julie looked to me and asked me why I was being so weird today. All I could respond with was that I had flashbacks of the time I was there as a kid and wanted to be in that moment again. Luckily, she believed me and told me to lie down if I wasn't feeling well, but I insisted on staying awake. Like usual, I lost the fight, so I went into the bedroom and lay down.

As I was lying in the room, all I kept doing was staring up at the ceiling, pondering on what I've seen today and all the questions I kept asking over and over, such as, why do I keep making a big deal out of those names? Have I seen those initials somewhere before? Why can't I just get over the idea that it's normal? Have I seen those before? All I kept doing was telling myself it was normal and telling myself it wasn't weird. As I kept fighting with my mind, eventually, I fell asleep.

Chapter Four:

I awoke from my nap and realized I was drenched in sweat. I awoke from a bad dream. A nightmare that seemed all too real. The dream was about the table and the building next to the lake. Even in my dreams, my mind was fighting with me, as it was when I was awake. This time it was like I was the one building the shed. I was a couple years younger and was wearing jeans, boots, and a flannel, like a construction worker would. I had measurement tools and handyman tools with me. There was a blueprint of the building laid out at my side, giving me an outline of what the building should look like. The man in my dream went to work building the shed-garage-looking thing and worked nonstop, not taking a break, not even to smoke a cig or to take a piss. The man in my dream was supposed to be me but the way he worked didn't match the way I would do things. He was different from me and that's what bothered me the most. It was like I knew him all too well and at the same time I didn't know him at all. This dream bothered me more than the names on the table did. He wasn't doing anything wrong, just creating a building. Unfortunately, I awoke when he finished the building and nothing about those names appeared in my dream. I couldn't figure out why this dream bothered me so much or even why I dreamt it, but it probably had something to do with me seeing all that earlier today, so it was still fresh in my mind down to the simplest detail.

I walked to the bathroom, got a glass of water, and splashed water on my face to wash away all the cold sweat that I woke to. I walked out into the living room and saw everyone sitting around. It came to my attention that it was late; the sky outside the windows was black. I couldn't believe I stayed asleep that long. John looked at me and said sarcastically good morning sleeping beauty. I started to apologize for sleeping but was immediately stopped by Julie and she said it was fine and that they understood. It was amazing that no one noticed the cold sweat that drenched me, but then again, they don't notice much of anything.

I insisted on a fire outside since it was a beautiful night. I knew the stars would be out above us, blanketing the night sky. They always looked mesmerizing and amazing to just get lost in their gaze. The city sky has nothing on the country sky. It's not really the country but when I'm almost in the middle of nowhere, it's considered the country to me. All those stars in the sky are all spaced out, making everything look peaceful and calm. I can look up at the sky and stare at them for hours and get lost in my imagination. It was amazing how much firewood I still had at the cabin and was shocked how dry it still was under the blue tarp. I started making the fire, gathering up small sticks and old newspaper we had lying around. I made a barrier from the bigger logs and placed them around the sticks before I lit them. The flame started out small, but when I added the lighter fluid, the flame soared into the sky. As the flames rose towards the sky, I felt the warm heat slap across my face as I backed away. I stood back and stared into the flames like I was in a trance, staring helplessly as if the flames were pulling me in. I was finally freed from the trance when everyone came out with their chairs.

I sat down next to Julie, and John handed me a beer. The cold, refreshing taste soothed my thirst as my throat became dry from the heat caused by the flames. The bottle was ice cold in my hand and the mountains on the Coors Light bottle were a bright blue. The condensation from the bottle bothered my hand so I set the bottle down and wiped off my hands. I reached into my pocket and grabbed out my cigarettes. I pulled one out and lit it up. It was my first cig since I woke up, so I felt the head rush, enjoying the nicotine high.

As I was lighting my cig John pointed out that the fire was dimming and I should throw more wood in. He was right when I looked at the fire and the flames were in fact dying down and the heat started to disappear. I reached down to put another log on and grab some more newspaper. It was very odd, but the newspaper I grabbed was the same paper I threw out this morning. I had a puzzled look on my face and kept asking myself how it got there. I swore to myself that I had indeed thrown it out this morning and didn't think it was possible for it to be right in front of me.

I blinked a couple of times to make sure I wasn't seeing things, but it still was the same paper. I shook my head in disbelief and threw it into the fire. The headline of **The Hatchet Killer** started to burn away; the words started to drift apart from one another. The title became unnoticeable finally and I looked up to find that we had company walking up to us. I stood up and glanced their way and waited patiently for them to approach us. There was a young guy and girl around our age. The man was wearing shorts, a cutoff shirt, and sandals, while the girl was wearing blue jeans with holes, a blue tank top, and white flip-flops.

"Hey guys, sorry for interrupting your evening; we were just on a walk, ended up lost and ended up here." The guy said.

"It's alright. We're just relaxing around the fire on this beautiful night." I replied.

"My name is Jake, and this is my girlfriend, Lindsey."

"I'm Mike, this is my girlfriend Julie and that's John and his girlfriend Molly."

They took turns introducing each other and shaking hands with all of us. They looked like a couple of nice people and I figured that they weren't the Hatchet Killer because they seemed madly in love and seemed like harmless people, so I simply asked if they wanted a beer and wanted to sit and join us.

"Sure, that'll be great. We both love fires, but as long as we aren't intruding."

"No, not at all; please sit down. Here are a couple of cold ones the mountains are still blue; drink it while it's still ice cold."

It didn't take us long for all of us to start laughing and having a good time. We were all a few beers in when Jake asked us if we wanted to hear a campfire story.

"You guys want to hear a campfire story?"

"Sure, we love a good story!" Molly exclaimed.

"It's not a pleasant story so if it's too inappropriate, I won't tell it," he said.

"Jake please, not this story again." Lindsey cried out.

"It'll be fine if they want to hear it."

"Yeah, go ahead," John said interestedly.

"Alright." He said as he began his story. "It all started a couple years back; a strange man came up this way and lived far from the town. No one knew where he came from or where exactly he lived, but he didn't come to town that much, so no one knew his actual name. But his nickname haunted everyone in the town to this day. The name "The Hatchet Killer" haunted the minds of the people throughout the houses. It got so bad that there was an actual curfew that took place where people weren't allowed to be out past a certain time.

Bodies started showing up in the woods in different spots and not in the same spot. The heads were missing off the victims and the most interesting point was they were all girls. Every single victim was a woman; not a single guy was found. There's a shed not far from here that was rumored that he built and took his victims there to torture and slaughter them."

"Ok, Ok, that's enough," the girls all said at the same time. We don't want to hear anymore."

I even agreed that I didn't want to hear anymore, since my plan to keep them from finding out about that story failed. I didn't want them to hear about it and ruin their stay here. It was supposed to be relaxing here, but now that is ruined too.

"Sorry, I'm sorry I told you the story wouldn't be pleasant to hear but figured it would have been fun to tell around a campfire," he replied.

"Yeah, not something that was recent." Molly exclaimed.

"Once again, I'm sorry. Look, it was fun and all hanging with you and I'm sorry I upset you guys so we're going to go and leave you guys to your night."

"Yeah, we're going to call it a night as well its late and that story scared probably all of us." Julie said.

"Alright, good night." Jake said as they got up to leave.

We all headed back inside and let the fire go, as it'll extinguish itself over time. As I walked inside all I kept thinking about was that damn shed building. All I wanted to know was what was inside it. I knew it was probably dangerous to go at night, but my curiosity was killing me so badly. I created a plan to go check it out while everyone was asleep and sneak out before my curiosity indeed does kill me. I had my father's gun still at the cabin, so I knew I would have some protection with me if something did happen.

We all said good night to each other and Julie and I went into our room to lie down. Now all I had to do was lie and wait until the time was right to make my move to sneak out.

Chapter Five:

It seemed like forever to me to finally make my move but when I glanced over, Julie was sound asleep, so I carefully got up, slipped on my clothes quietly, and left the room.

I didn't want to create a lot of noise, so I moved as silently as possible. The training I had on moving silently was from years of practice when I used to sneak out of the house when I lived at home to go with my friends to late-night fires and nights full of drinking. I grabbed a flashlight while finding my boots and headed out the side door. The side door is the quietest door to sneak out of, since the other doors tend to creak when being opened, especially when being opened slowly. I was successful at perfecting opening and shutting the door without making a peep.

As I walked away from the cabin I looked up and noticed it was a clear night, not a cloud in the sky, just an oasis of stars scattered across the night sky. The moon was shining bright and giving me enough light to walk through the dark woods. I was never afraid of walking through the woods at night, especially with the light from the moon. It was just my luck it was a full moon, not a new moon, so I tucked away my flashlight and saved the batteries for the building next to the lake. I was taught when I was younger that fear is fear itself, so I always knew that everything else is just an illusion clouding someone's judgment from reality.

It was a cool night with whispering winds passing through the trees, shaking them slightly. The leaves didn't make any noise, probably quieter than I am leaving the cabin. I had on a flannel, so I didn't feel the breeze or the coolness from the air. The temperature was almost perfect, just the way I liked it. Opening your mind and listening to the background, it was as if there was nothing there. Not a single sound was coming from the forest, not even the sound of crickets or locusts, which I found very strange. But it was so peaceful, and my mind enjoyed the peace and quiet because it was racing a hundred miles an hour.

All I kept thinking about was the same question I thought about all day and all night: "What's in that building?" I feel like I know what's in there but can't recall anything. It all seems so familiar to me and that's what bothers me the most. Why does this all feel too real to me? Why can't I just let this go? The same questions kept popping into my mind as if trying to haunt me so I picked up my pace and walked quicker to the building.

The building finally came into sight and my heart dropped. Not from fear, but almost an excited sense of relief. I carefully checked out my surroundings to see if I caught any sight of people or, primarily, this killer out there. I looked around twice, didn't see any movement and walked up to the building itself. I walked around and checked the perimeter to find no sign of anything. I went up to the door and tried to open it but it wouldn't budge. It was locked. I checked the windows and they too were bolted shut.

I stepped back and thought long and hard about how to get inside. I reached into my pocket and grabbed out my cabin key and figured it would have been a long shot but wanted to try it anyway. I put the key inside the keyhole just to be let down; there was no luck the key fit but it wouldn't turn. There was another cabin key my father gave me and didn't know the purpose for it. I always thought it was in the gun safe inside the cabin. So, I decided to try that key out as well. If that didn't work, I would never figure out what's inside, and I wasn't about to break the window to get inside. I inserted the key into the lock and to my astonishment, the key worked, and the door unlocked. Now the next question that ran through my head was: was it my father who built this here and I don't remember him doing so?

I slowly entered the door and pulled out my flashlight. I took a quick glance to make sure no one was inside but to my luck, it was empty. I walked around and glanced at everything to see what's inside. There was a table in the middle of the room with straps at its side. The table was made out of steel. It was very clean, showing the glistening moonlight on its sanitized, polished surface. The table was cool to the touch. I had no idea what use it was for because there was no fish the size of the table. Next to the table a cart was filled with tools and was ready to be used. The tools were made from steel as well and they too were very clean. They looked like doctors' equipment used for surgery and yet, again, were not used for fish. A chill ran down my back because what I saw so far was way too sketchy. I walked over to the table against the wall and noticed that it seemed normal due to its wooden texture and all the everyday tools needed in a shed, except for the tools you'll need while you're at the lake.

On the wall above the table were more tools. Weird tools at that, tools that don't fit and don't belong, but then again, nothing here actually belonged. The weirdest thing that I came across was a filing cabinet. What is the purpose of having a filing cabinet all the way out here next to a body of water? I opened the filing cabinet and came across tabs with different labels that included **Pictures, Backgrounds,**

IDs, and Health Records. The labels were very disturbing but also very intriguing. Instead of being disgusted, I became more interested.

I went through each label, starting with IDs; I didn't want to look at the pictures yet because I didn't want to be disturbed—I was just curious. The names that came out noticeably were the initials I'd seen before. A.S. R.A. L.W T.Y. The initials that were engraved in the table just outside the building. Those were only a few of the names; there were many more IDs in here as well. I moved to the "Background" label and the papers inside were detailed reports on the lives of the individual's initials found inside. Even their health records were found on them as well. Someone must have had a way of getting the info from somewhere. Or has a source to get the info. Either way there was a lot of personal information on these individuals that was disturbingly interesting.

I prepared myself to look at the file named "Pictures" because something seemed off. The pictures shown were of the girls in the other files, with their initials written on the back of them. Then the pictures went to a whole other level. Pictures of the girls being tortured were taken with everything being done to them. Pictures of the girls on the table, with the tools being used. Girls tied up against the wall in the building, and girls that looked awfully beaten. I threw the pictures down and shut the filing cabinet. As I was getting myself ready to leave, I came to notice something else.

There was a drawer on the wooden table by the tools and I opened it up to look inside. My curiosity was killing me. As I opened the drawer, I saw things that gave me instant flashbacks and even more chills. There were items inside that looked like they were mine. Pens that were mine sat inside the drawer and my initials were engraved in the wood as well. Along with other things that were mine, they were found inside.

There was clothing that was mine inside the building and I became even more uncomfortable at that time.

I know for a fact I was never inside this place before, but my clothes were here, my initials were here, and the pens I used, with my initials on them, were inside the drawer. It all came at me too fast and the confusion was destroying my mind.

Chapter Six:

The next morning came, and the sun blazed into the room. Once again, I was alone in the bedroom. I awoke with confusion racing through my mind. I decided to take another morning shower to de-stress myself. I managed to get myself out of bed and stood in the shower, letting the water run on my skin. I still don't exactly know what was going on. Instead of getting all the answers my curious mind wanted, I got even more questions. I thought to myself that Frank probably knew more about this Hatchet Killer campfire story than the kids that I met yesterday.

Frank isn't the oldest person in town, obviously, but he has been around for a long time and he's the only one that would be honest with me. I figured after breakfast I would go see him alone. I don't want to scare everyone again after yesterday.

After I made up my mind to go visit Frank, I finished with my shower. I turned off the water, got out, and dried myself off. I walked back into the bedroom to put my clothes on. I then walked towards the kitchen. This time it wasn't cheesy eggs but waffles and sausage. The smell was still amazing with the mixture between the pancake mix, syrup and the browning of the sausage.

I glanced at Julie, gave her a smile and then a kiss and simply told her good morning.

"Good morning." Julie replied as she leaned in to give me a kiss.

"Looks great." I said excitedly.

"Thank you! How'd you sleep?" She asked.

"Great!" As I lied to cover up the info I found last night. "I want to go visit Frank again today."

"Why's that?" She asked curiously.

"Oh, he's a family friend and we didn't have much time to catch up yesterday."

"Okay, just don't be gone too long. I want to spend time with you."

"I won't take long, just want to see how he's been."

"Do you want some coffee?"

"Yes, but can I take it to go?"

She reached up into the cupboard and pulled out a travel mug and poured the coffee into it. I didn't want to be rude, so I finished the plate of food she made for me. The waffles were fluffy, and the sausage was cooked to perfection with a nice golden-brown color to it. As I finished, I put the plate in the sink, gave Julie another kiss, and left.

I left the cabin and headed into town to Frank's shop. The morning sun was out, giving off a nice wave of heat along with a slight breeze. Again, there weren't many people out giving off that eerie feeling. It didn't take long to reach the old shop. As I approached, Frank was standing out front unlocking the store.

"Hey there Mike, good morning," Frank said, coughing into his handkerchief.

"Good morning Frank." I responded.

"What gives me the pleasure so early?"

"I wanted to come by and ask a question that's been bothering me."

"Oh? And what's that?"

"It's about this killer." I responded anxiously.

"Well now, I'm sure you've heard the story by now."

"I have, but I feel like there's more to it."

"Hmm, well, you're right about that. How about you come inside, so we can talk about it."

We walked into the shop as he unlocked the door, and we walked towards the back of the store to what looked like a break room. The room also looked like a storeroom with boxes of shit stacked on top of one another. There were shelves along the other wall with papers and dusty knickknacks of all sorts. The table where we were going to sit was in the middle of the semi-small room. It was a small round table with two barstools at its sides.

"You want some more coffee?" He asked as he headed towards the coffeepot.

"Yeah, sure. I can use some more." I replied, handing him my travel mug.

"You want some strong shit in it?"

"No, just creamer," I laughed.

"Here you go." He handed back the mug as he reached into his vest pocket and pulled out a flask. "It'll put some hair on your chest." He added as he chuckled.

As he chuckled, it caused him to cough even more. He pulled out his handkerchief to cough into it. I'm assuming some nasty shit came out as he did so.

"Now, what exactly do you want to know?" He asked as he finally sat down on the other stool.

"Well, I heard the story people tell around the campfire, but I feel like there's more to the story I haven't heard yet. I feel like there's more history than what I've heard so far."

"History?" He coughed.

"Yeah, the history behind the story."

"Yup there is an origin behind the spooky tale. You got the time for it?"

"I got some time. The question is, do you? Running this store and all?"

"Hell, I haven't had a customer in quite some time." He chuckles and coughs some more.

"Well, we'll start from the very beginning. So, there was this mine not far from here and a small town sort of like this one. When the mine was functioning, the town prospered till there was ncthing left in the mine. It shut down and operations had to move. Once the operations moved, most of the town moved as well to work elsewhere. The other part stayed for a little while but eventually had to move as well since they ran out of resources.

Many people know of this part of the history already. I used to live in that town. I didn't want to move far away, so I just moved over here. The part of the story not known to many is the part about Dr. Jacob Underwood.

Dr. Underwood was a very smart man. He was the town's doctor that did it all. He worked on animals and humans. He took care of a simple cold and a complicated surgery. He was a well-respected man in town; everyone loved the guy. Sounds alright so far, huh? He asked, looking at me as I shook my head in agreement.

The story so far isn't all that bad, but a few years passed and people started to disappear. The local authorities did a search and an investigation but couldn't come up with anything. Everything was quiet during the investigation, until they decided to call it off. A couple weeks went by, and more people turned up missing.

The authorities still couldn't solve this puzzling mystery. One day, a townsman saw Dr. Underwood and someone else go into his house and never come back out. I'm not sure if that townsman had any sense that something was off with the doctor, but he decided to stay and keep an eye on Dr. Underwood.

As the man kept watch on the doctor, he saw another person walk into the house with Underwood. The man waited patiently, and to his suspicion, they never came back out.

The townsman saw enough and gathered some townsfolk for a meeting. He provided his findings to the gathering, and all decided to take matters into their own hands. They all agreed to storm Dr. Underwood's house that same night. They raced over there with firearms and flashlights.

As the townsfolk reached Underwood's house, they all snuck inside. The house was very spotless and cleaned to perfection. They searched the entire house and came up empty until they found the door to the cellar.

They crept down the stairs, and their eyes grew big. As they looked around, they saw chains hanging from the ceiling; hooks dangling, such as the ones used to hoist up animals in a butcher's shop; and various tools hanging on the walls. These tools ranged from saws, hammers, drills, and knives. Closer to the back of the room, surgical tools were on a small stand in uniform order.

The smell was very vile and had a rotten stench to it. The smell of decay filled the room and lingered in your nose forever. The sight of blood was still fresh all over the walls and floors of the cellar.

Dr. Underwood stood facing one of his latest victims with a scalpel in his hand. The townsfolk charged at him, tying him up, while the others had their guns drawn on him."

"How do you know all of this?" I asked, interrupting him.

"Cause I was one of those town folks holding a gun at him. I was very young at the time but knew how to shoot if I needed to." He replied as he continued the story.

"Now, after we tied him up, we didn't turn him over for his crimes. Instead, we took him down into the mine and locked him up there. We were going to starve his ass to death.

Here's where the story gets even more interesting. As we all thought he would die down there of starvation, it turns out he didn't. Somehow he had escaped, but he never returned.

One day a traveler came across a body in the woods, which was later identified as Underwood's body. At this point that old town was abandoned, and this town was doing well.

A few years have passed, and it was very quiet until bodies started disappearing again. So, then another legend started to spread. Some of the villagers that lived over by the mine moved to this town and started up a new story. This story explained that they felt Dr. Underwood put a curse of some sort into the woods.

The curse of Dr. Underwood was said to be his spirit that searches for a new host to quench the thirst to kill. The anger of the spirit was so bad that many that have come up here turned up missing."

"So why the people stay up here then? Why don't they just leave?" I asked puzzled.

"It's not that easy; even those who tried to leave vanished before they got anywhere." He explained.

"So, let me get this straight. There was a doctor that tortured patients; he was then caught, left for dead, ended up escaping, and died anyways, but before dying, cursed the woods to have his spirit take over someone else's to continue killing for him?"

"So, the legend says," Frank replied.

"Do you believe all that?"

"Gives an answer to all this Hatchet Killer persona."

"I guess," I replied with a shrug.

"Anyways, that's the story and the history that you asked for, is there anything else that you need help with?"

"No, that helped amazingly." I answered, still in disbelief of the whole situation.

"Well, I hope to see you around again kid. For now I got to clean up the shop and hope a paying customer comes in."

"I thank you for the time, Frank." I said as I got up from the table to leave his shop.

I walked out of the shop, and my mind was racing more now than it ever had, if that was even possible. I then headed back to the cabin to spend time with Julie and my friends.

Chapter Seven:

As I got back to the cabin, everyone was just hanging around. They were all sitting in the living room as I walked in, planning the afternoon activities.

"What shall we do today?" John asked.

"Mike, you have any ideas?" Julie asked.

"Ummm…" I paused as I spaced out. "Not sure, anything, really."

"How about a scary movie marathon?" Molly asked happily.

Everyone turned and agreed. We all got cozy on the couch and turned on the Blu-ray player. We popped on a collection of Classic Horror Films and the first movie that played was Dracula.

As the movie played, I decided to build a fire in the fireplace beside the TV. After a few moments I finally got it up and running, really setting the mood.

The fire burned for a while as the movie kept playing. Almost halfway through the movie, everyone was falling asleep. Everyone except for me, as my mind continued to race. All I wanted to do was to head back to the shed and continue looking for clues as to what the hell was going on.

I waited a little longer and when I noticed everyone passed out, I decided to sneak out once again. I decided to sneak out the same way I did last night. I finally got up and headed to the side door, slid it open and left.

As I left, the sun started to set. We must have been out of it for a while, well, everyone except me; I just couldn't control my mind. I headed back down the path towards the shed. The evening was quiet and calm. There wasn't a sound being made.

I reached the shed and pulled out my key to unlock it. I walked through the door and took a deep breath, preparing myself for what to expect this time. I sat down on the chair and opened the filing cabinet once more.

I decided this time to go to the oldest file in the cabinet and pulled it out. To my astonishment, on the back of the files, the initials J.U. were found on the bottom. Now that I knew what J.U. stood for, everything came together. I guess that old man was telling the truth. I thought to myself. But how did his files end up here? Why do I have access to them?

I didn't get to think about it much because I heard a noise coming from outside. The noise of voices. I crept outside the building to hide in the shadows. As the voices came closer, I realized it was the couple from earlier. They seemed drunk or stoned from the way they walked and talked. Evidence of beer in their hands was apparent as well. I kept perfectly still and quiet as I just watched them walk on by, not caring about their surroundings.

It wouldn't have mattered if I made noise or not because they seemed too out of it to even care. They began to run and as they were running they started to take their clothes off to go for a midnight skinny-dipping session. As I saw them go into the water all of a sudden, my mind seemed to shut off and all I could see was red.

It was a very strange feeling to me. My mind stopped working and it almost felt like I was going to black out. Instead, all I saw was red. As if blood were filling my eyes. I don't have any recognition of feeling this way before.

It feels as if I don't have control over my mind. In fact, I don't. My mind seems like it has taken control over me. It seems like I'm in a dream—no, a bad dream—and I can't wake myself up from it.

My heart started to speed up, and the feeling of hate boiled my blood. My face has gotten so hot, to the point I was sweating in my flannel. My eyes perked up when I caught a glimpse of the two in the water.

I looked over and noticed the guy getting out of the water. He looked back over his shoulder and cried out,

"I'll be right back; just got to take a piss. Don't go anywhere without me."

Suddenly, I turned around and went back inside of the building. It still feels like I have no control of what I was doing, but it was all too real. I went over and grabbed one of the steel knives. It felt cool in my hands as I gripped the knife tightly. I walked back out and saw the guy by the tree.

As I crept closer, I could hear him singing to himself as he pissed on the tree. He's focused on not falling over and making sure that he hits all of it on the tree. At this point I was right behind him, noticing he still hasn't noticed anything going on in his surroundings.

I placed my hand over his mouth and took the knife in the other hand and jabbed it into his throat. I took a step back and noticed the look he gave me as he struggled to catch his last few breaths and tried to stop his throat from bleeding out. The sounds of garbling from the blood filling and leaving his throat were all you heard. His hands kept moving about on his throat, trying to hopelessly save himself. His eyes bulged hugely as the pain and shock formed. He fell to his knees and at this point it was over. It was too late for him; within seconds, he fell to the ground, dead from blood loss. I reached down to grab the knife and held on to it.

I looked over at the lake to notice the girl was still in the water, clueless as to what had happened. Then, I hear,

"Babe, Hurry up! I'm lonely in here."

I watched her get out of the water. She was fully naked as she ran to her clothes. She managed to put her underwear and her shirt back on by the time I came up behind her. I grabbed her, threw her to the ground, and covered her mouth so she didn't scream. I was twice her size, so holding her down wasn't a problem. I then put the duct tape over her mouth and tied her up with the rope I brought.

I lifted her up over my shoulder like a sack of potatoes. She started kicking and squirming around trying to escape. All I heard coming from her was the muttering,

"Mmm-hmm."

She couldn't get anything else out of her mouth, Since I had the tape tightly over her mouth. I kicked open the door to the building and set her on the table with the straps. I strapped her down and took the rope off but kept the tape over her mouth. I looked at her face and her eyes were opened wide but covered in tears.

I left the girl lying on the table as I went out back by the lake. I searched the area and found her purse. I tossed around everything until I found her ID. I grabbed the ID and walked back to the building. I walked over to the table and grabbed a camera. I took a picture of the girl and wrote her initials on the back. I then threw the picture and ID in the correct places.

After I put the items away, I took another glance at the girl to see her in the same terrified way I left her, and suddenly, I couldn't see anything. It was as if my mind had shut completely off or I had finally blacked out.

Chapter Eight:

Out of nowhere, I jumped up from my sleep. Sweat was pouring down my face, and my shirt was soaked. I wasn't wearing my flannel anymore and didn't have pants on. All I was wearing was a black t-shirt and a pair of boxers.

The room was normal, and my girlfriend was still sound asleep, not noticing my gasps for air or that I awoke from a bad dream. It all felt so real for it to be just a dream though, I thought to myself. But there was no evidence that I even left.

I decided to go take a shower so I could switch out of the soaked shirt. As I stood in the shower, the thoughts from my realistic dream popped into my head. The only thing that sucked was the images in my head stopped at the point of the girl crying. That was the last thing I remembered from the dream.

There was only one thing to do, and that was to go down to the lake and see if it was just a bad dream or not. The thought of finding out the truth really bothered me. I wanted to be sure that it was just a bad dream and not reality.

The water felt nice and I didn't want to get out. I knew I'd have time to go down by the lake before anyone woke up. So, I turned the water off, dried off, and got dressed. There wasn't anyone up, so I snuck out the side door and made my way down to the lake.

First, I looked by where the guy in my dream was peeing by. To my astonishment, I found nothing. A sigh of relief came from my lips as I was glad to find nothing wrong. My next worry was the girl in the building. The whole way to the building I was nervous and worried I'd see her in there, still crying and strapped down.

I hesitated to open the door; when I finally did, I didn't see any sign that anything had taken place there. The table with the straps was clean. The steel shone from the moonlight coming through the window, gleaming down on it. I started to calm down a bit and noticed that everything in my dream was true except for the guy and the girl so far. All the details were spot on. So, I learned a few details from the dream, especially those of the files.

Looking back into my dream I remembered the file labels and the two items that were placed in them. If there is anything in that cabinet that corresponds to my dream, I'd for sure freak out. It was very freaky how everything in this room was exactly how my dream portrayed it. As if it weren't a dream at all.

This time my hands started to shake as I approached the filing cabinet. I took long breaths, too nervous to open the drawer. After a few seconds I opened the drawer with my eyes closed shut. I then opened them to see the files marked exactly how they were in my dream. The next things to check were the only two items that had been filed away: the I.D. and the picture of the girl.

Once again, I hesitated before going through the files. I started with the file that was marked I.D.S. First, I started with wishing that girl wasn't in there, but with my luck, she was. I jumped back, startled. A part of me started to freak out, but the other part of me wanted to look at the picture's file.

I thumbed through the pictures and every girl that was in my dream was in there and the last picture in the file was the girl that was strapped down on the table. That picture wasn't the only picture of that girl. Horrible pictures followed next. Images that shouldn't be explained were paper-clipped together. She was horribly tortured and misconfigured.

With that, I threw the files back into the cabinet and ran out of the building. As I ran back to the cabin, all I kept thinking about was, " What happened to the bodies? What happened to the guy and girl in my dream? And, Did I really do that?"

The jog back to the cabin wasn't pleasant. All the questions ran through my head. There was no way I had anything to do with what happened to those two. There was no way I could do any of that when I was at the cabin sleeping.

As I returned to the cabin, Molly was in the kitchen like normal, cooking breakfast.

"Where did you go?" She asked, looking at me.

"Oh, I went for a run." I lied as sweat poured down my face.

"Got to keep in shape even on a vacation?"

"Yes, ma'am," I said, managing to laugh.

"You want some coffee?"

"Yes, hot and black, you know me," I replied.

"No problem." As she handed me a cup with very hot coffee. Then she says, "By the way here's the paper."

"Thank you." I said as I took the paper out of her hand.

I took the paper out of the bag and opened it up. Sure enough, the Hatchet Killer made the front cover. To my astonishment, there was a front story about another victim killed. It read:

Another girl was found last night in the woods. The head was missing just like the rest of the victims. The Hatchet Killer strikes again, it seems. Local Police are still trying to figure out the identity of the female. They are not giving us much now.

A part of me already knew who that female was, but the other part of me wanted to ignore any knowledge of it. I still can't get over what happened to that couple. Everything in my dream was accurate except how the girl died or where the bodies even went. The main question kept running through my mind: "How did it all happen, and was I in any way a part of it?" I wanted to believe that maybe I had this power to bring an end to the killer, and maybe that's why I had the dream, but that seemed unreasonable.

At this point my head was swimming and I just wanted to take my mind off things for a little while.

Chapter Nine:

As I lay in the room, my mind raced even faster. I couldn't control it or at least slow it down. It didn't take long for me to finally doze off, since my mind had pretty much worn itself out.

I started to sink deep down into my unconsciousness and seemed like everything started spinning even in my dream. It looked like a wormhole I was headed down, with the spinning, swirling, and changing colors.

Suddenly, my unconscious mind came to a complete stop, ending the trippy adventure. As the dream started to become clear, I saw myself standing in front of the lake shed. I was staring at the door feeling strangely different. All these strange emotions wouldn't be the ones I would normally express.

I had feelings of anger, pain, and hatred mixed with pure excitement. My skin felt hot, very hot, almost like I had a very bad fever. Even though I didn't feel sick, my blood was boiling and all I could see was red.

My hands were no longer shaking as I finally reached for the door handle. I felt so confident, not trembling with my emotions. I walked inside the shed and turned on the lights.

I moved toward the coat rack in the corner of the room and put on what seemed like a lab coat. I then moved over to the sink and began washing my hands. I threw on a pair of surgical gloves and turned towards the steel table. I turned on the light near the table and opened the curtain that blocked the view.

To my astonishment, the girl is lying there strapped down. At this point, I no longer had control over my own mind; this new mind had complete control. The straps were over her wrists and ankles, completely secure—no way for her to move or get out.

The girl had tape over her mouth, muffling her cries. There were tears pouring down her face, eyes wide with fear. I moved closer to her face and just stared at her eyes, trying to get them bigger than what they already are.

I stood there for a few moments and took in all the emotions I was feeling. I grabbed a scalpel and ran it up and down her body, making her cry some more. Her breathing was getting faster as I inserted the scalpel into her cheek. I made a tiny cut and suddenly, the girl passed out, probably from fear and anxiety.

This pissed me off. How was I supposed to feel anything if she passed out? I grabbed a water bottle, splashed it on her face, and then slapped her face hard.

As she woke back up, it took her a minute to figure out where she was again. I didn't want her to pass out again, so I grabbed a syringe filled with lidocaine, but a very strong dose of it. I wanted to make sure she couldn't feel anything, so she didn't pass out again. I then grabbed two eye instruments and put them on her eyelids. I wanted to secure the fact that she couldn't close her eyes.

The horror in her eyes was to the extreme. I continued to use the scalpel all over her body, making cut marks on her skin, and watching the blood drip down into the stainless pan underneath the table.

I started to get bored using the scalpel and wanted to use something else. I walked over to the cabinet and grabbed a ball-peen hammer. I held it in my hand, feeling the cool steel coming through the gloves.

I walked back over to the table and took a moment to stare at the girl. She was still in fear and shock, eyes wide open, tears running down her face. The blood continued to run down her face, and then down her naked body.

After I took in the moment, I then took my time wailing down certain areas on her body. Hearing the crunching of the bones breaking, causing more blood to come out. I hit as many places as I wanted to repeatedly until I got bored with that.

I'd reached the point where torture no longer gave me that sense of satisfaction. The problem I always had was that, since she couldn't feel the pain, I didn't get to hear any anguish. I decided to wait till the strong dose of lidocaine wore off so the feeling of pain could once more flow through her body.

In the meantime, I grabbed my camera and took pictures of the work I've accomplished. I waited a little while for the lidocaine to wear off, and shortly after, I heard the pain and anguish race through her body and emotions. Tears flowed more than ever. The sound of her attempted screams trying to escape the duct tape was so strong that it was as if she didn't have any tape over her mouth at all.

I took in all these exciting feelings for a short while. I finally thought it was time to reach for my hatchet. I put down the camera and filed away the pictures after putting down initials on the back. I reached for the hatchet and walked back to the table. I stood over her, sort of mocking her, and prepared to strike the hatchet down over her throat.

The sounds of muffled "Please don't. No!" came out of the girl when I finally struck down, severing the head. I learned to carefully blow to sever the head off the body; that way it's not sloppy or messy. The less mess to clean, the better the chance of covering up the crime.

The moment I reached down to pick up the head from the floor, my mind again started to race. It felt like I was returning down that wormhole that I once went down in the beginning. My eyes began to blur until they went dark. I couldn't see anything. Everything went blank.

Chapter Ten:

I jolted up wide awake, sweat pouring down my body. I'm starting to get over waking up like this. Every time I wake up, it's sudden and I'm drenched. It's a surprise how Julie hasn't noticed that I do this all the time. My mind was racing at full capacity. I sat up in bed, moved my legs to touch the cold floor and tried to shake off the emotions I was having. My head felt heavy from all the questions, flashbacks, and images from my dreams. My realistic trippy dreams.

At this point I no longer have any control over my mind whatsoever. I didn't feel the same. This was no longer my mind to control. My head continued to pound and my eyes were burning. I finally stood up out of bed. The coolness from the floor felt great on my bare feet. The anxious, confused state of my mind caused me to pace around the room. I started to pace faster and faster, my head pounding harder and harder. I took my hands and grabbed my head. It felt like something was inside, crawling around causing all the terrible throbs. The dream I had felt more like a memory than anything. That was the part that was troublesome. It scared the shit out of me, making my dream feel like a reality that I wanted no part in.

As I continued to pace back and forth, the confusion started to clear, making my thoughts come together, but the thoughts were no longer mine. The thoughts became one with my emotions. I was a new man. No longer my old self.

I made my way to the bathroom and turned on the faucet. I splashed water on my face continuously and stared into the mirror. The longer I stared into the mirror feeling of hate and anger filled my entire body. The feeling of anger coursed through me, boiling my skin. The uncontrolled anger that I once felt before in what I thought was a dream was once more alive, stronger than ever. I have no idea why I was so angry, but the feeling started to feel great, as if I were accepting this emotion.

The anger turned into a need. This need was the need to kill again. I felt as if I were an addict waiting for my next fix. My body and mind craved the feeling of having complete control over someone, watching them fear for their lives. My head hasn't stopped pounding and my ears felt clogged. There was a voice that popped in my mind, a deep, demanding voice that repeated the same words: "Kill, Kill, Kill, Kill." Then I started to think about who would be my next victim: "Who's Next?"

The voice continued, "Take the next victim slower. I need to feel the full thrill of the ride." I shook my head, splashed some more water on my face and glanced back in the mirror. Only I didn't see myself. My reflection wasn't what I saw. The reflection that appeared was of an older man. The man presented himself as clean-cut. Clean-cut salt-n-pepper beard with a short top of matching hair on top of his head. Glasses sat on the bridge of his nose. The fire in his eyes pierced back at me. With the glare and my mind going a hundred miles an hour, I let out a surprised scream.

I didn't think the scream was loud, but before I knew it, Julie raced up the stairs and into the bathroom.

"What's wrong? What happened?" She asked, full of concern.

"It was just a bad dream." I lied as my breathing sounded heavy and fast.

"What about?" She asked.

"I'm not sure, honestly." I replied back, continuing the lie. "I Just want to forget about it."

"Okay." She responded, sounding soothing.

As the reality in front of me started to come back, I placed my hands over my eyes and shook my head. This is starting to get out of hand. I peeked another glance in the mirror, but this time I saw my own reflection, noticing the white face of a terrified man.

Chapter Eleven:

I left the bathroom feeling flushed in the face. The feeling of exhaustion poured over me. I haven't had a solid night's sleep since I got here. My face felt hot, and I'm sure it was beet red. I wiped sweat off my brow as I sat on the edge of the bed. To my astonishment, Julie was no longer in the room, giving me a moment to recollect my thoughts. I sat there for a few moments not thinking of anything for the first time in a while. The clock on the wall grew louder and louder, each tick of the second hand echoing in my ears. Listening to the tick, ticK, tiCK, tICK, TICK, then I came to feel parched. Thirst poured into my thoughts, and all I truly wanted was a drink.

I sat up on the edge of the bed and made my way out of the room. Sweat still fell down my face, still feeling hot. I walked slowly down the steps, headed to the kitchen. I looked around and saw the girls sitting around the table.

"Hey babe." Julie said as I approached.

"Hey." I said wearily.

"Are you okay?" She asked worriedly. "You look exhausted."

"I'm fine," I lied. "Just overheated and real thirsty."

"Want some water hon?" Julie asked, about to rise from the chair.

"No. I need something other than water." I mustered up a laugh.

"That's what I'm talking about." Molly exclaimed.

"I feel like you can use some water." Julie said protectively.

"I could use both." Surprisingly, sounding stern with a sharp attitude.

"Okay." Julie said short.

"I'm sorry it's got to be the heat making me short-tempered." I said as I grabbed her and gave her a hug.

As I stood there hugging her, I glanced over her shoulder, seeing Molly stare at me with suspicious looks. She gave me a sly smile like she was up to something. I gave Julie a kiss and walked over to the fridge to grab a bottle of water.

"How about this?" I began, uncapping the bottle. "We all go down by the lake for a dip, and I'll drink water till we get there."

"Okay, deal. I can work with that." Julie responds agreeably. "But I'm planning on making dinner tonight, so I won't stay late. I won't stop your fun though. It'll give me time to prepare the food while y'all are still enjoying yourselves."

"Oh, what do you have planned?" I asked curiously.

"It's a surprise." She said smirking.

"I'll go and see if John wants to come along and get ready." Molly said as she started walking away.

Julie left right after Molly to go get herself ready. I stayed behind to finish the bottle of water I took out of the fridge. I moved towards the trash can to throw out the empty bottle and headed to the stairs to get a pair of swim trunks on. As I moved upstairs, I stopped by Molly and John's room, curious to see if he was coming with us or not, but all I saw was Molly in the room.

I stopped and peered through the crack in the door. The door was left open on purpose, it seems. Through the crack, I can see Molly through the mirror in the corner of the room. I watched as she shimmied off her shorts and bent over to pull on her bikini bottoms. The white bottom looked amazing on her toned, tanned ass as she admired herself in the mirror. She turned and took her shirt off, baring her tits with her hard nipples. Her breasts were perfectly formed as she put her matching bikini top on, tying the strings behind her back. As she stretched her elbows back, her breasts popped out forward, making them fully noticeable. I saw her twirl back and forth, staring at her body as she approved of the way she looked. I stayed for a few more minutes, until she slid her tight shorts back on, struggling to get them over her round, toned buttocks.

I turned to leave the cracked door, heading to my room as I shook my head in disappointment. Not in a million years would I ever do that. I have no idea what came over me. I love Julie too much to even notice other women. What has been happening to me lately has completely changed me as a person. At the same time, I couldn't help but think how lucky John was to have a piece of ass like that.

I was about to enter my room as Julie came out, already dressed. If I stayed out of Molly's room even a moment longer, I would have a lot of explaining to do.

"Hey babe." Julie exclaimed, seeing me.

"Hey," I responded. "You're all dressed and ready?"

"Yes, I'm good to go," Julie answered.

"Okay, I'm just going to throw on swim trunks really quick and I'll be down."

She turned and headed down the stairs as I searched for my swim trunks, leaving the door open since it wouldn't take me long to put them on. I took off the bottoms I was wearing along with my boxers and grabbed my trunks. To my surprise, out of the corner of my eye, I saw Molly at my door, doing the same thing I was doing to her. I saw her eyes fall down my body to my half erection; thanks to her anyway. I pretended like she wasn't there and slowly put my trunks on. As I tied the trunks tight, I caught her turning to leave, smiling.

I threw on a shirt and left the room, heading down the stairs. As I approached the kitchen, I saw the girls at the table once again.

"Is John joining us?" I asked as I approached.

"No," Molly replied. "He said he wanted to focus on working out."

"Let me guess," I said, staring at the girls. "Gotta stay in shape for the season even on vacation." I said in a mocking tone.

"Yeah, that's pretty much what he said." Molly agreed, laughing at my imitation.

We grabbed a couple bottles of wine, and I grabbed a few bottles of water to honor my deal. I tossed the bottles in a bag, and we all headed out the door.

Chapter Twelve:

Molly, Julie, and I headed out the door towards the trail to the lake. As promised, I drank water as we walked down the trail. The weather outside was gorgeous. It was a beautiful 82 degrees out, with the sun still shining. It was getting later in the afternoon, but even when the sun sets, it'll still be about 75 degrees out. Looking up at the trees surrounding the path, there was a slight breeze making them sway back and forth a little.

I continued to drink more water, just to say I'd had plenty, aching for some wine. It seemed like the closer we got, the thirstier I became. Sweat continued to run down my face as my face continued to burn. After what seemed like forever, we neared the picnic table, relieved that we were finally at the lake.

"Finally!" I explained. "Time to drink."

I heard Molly laugh with excitement, and Julie sighed with annoyance. I set the bag down on the table and pulled out a bottle of wine and my portable speaker. I grabbed a cork opener and some plastic cups. I handed one to Molly, kept one for myself, and when I was about to hand one to Julie, she waved me off.

"No thanks." She expressed. "I'll have something to drink at dinner; for now, water is fine."

"Party pooper," Molly joked.

"Come on now," I said supportively. "She's about to make us all dinner."

"Exactly," Julie agreed jokingly.

I sipped on my wine and hooked up the speaker.

"What shall we listen to?" I asked.

"I'm feeling a little rock. Something exciting." Julie answered.

I saw Molly bob her head in agreement, and I turned on my rock mix. The first song that came on was *Something in Your Mouth* by Nickelback. I turned the volume up and saw Molly start dancing, sipping on her wine. She looked sexy, swaying back and forth in her bikini. Her toned ass moving back and forth. Her firm tits bouncing up and down. It was hard to keep your eyes off the hard body. Meanwhile, Julie looked boring, not interested in anything. I kept pounding my wine while listening to the music. The next song that came on was Closer, by Nine Inch Nails, and I continued to watch Molly feel the music.

"I feel like it's finally time to jump in the water." Molly said, still dancing and sipping her wine.

"I think I'm just going to head back and start on dinner." Julie responded.

"Awh, really? We haven't even gotten in the water yet." I exclaimed.

"I want to get dinner started before it gets too late. You guys can go in and continue to have fun. I should have dinner about ready when you guys are done," Julie said confidently.

"Okay," I said, giving her a hug and a kiss, watching her turn to head back to the cabin.

"Well, I think it's time to head into the water." Molly said.

I gathered up the speaker and the bottle of wine and walked down to the dock leading towards the lake. The weather was still perfect outside. A slight breeze, with warm air, fills the atmosphere. I set the bottle down while Molly carried our glasses.

"I'm so excited for this." Molly exclaimed.

"Too bad John isn't here enjoying this with us." I expressed.

"Yeah, but how often do the two of us get some quality time together to let loose and not be on guard?" Molly asked.

"Fair enough." I answered with a smirk.

Molly couldn't wait any longer and ran down the dock to jump into the lake. I continued to sip on my wine while I watched her run, her toned ass jiggling as she ran. Her bikini bottom was going farther up her crack. She turned behind her, asking if I was coming. I assured her I'd be right behind her. I wanted to make sure everything was where it should be and that we'd be able to hear the music. After everything was placed in its spot, I walked down the dock to dip my toes in the water.

"Come on, the water feels amazing." Molly whined.

As I dipped my toes in the water, I confirmed Molly's observation and jumped in. The water was indeed perfect. The water wasn't too cold. It was the perfect warm temperature from the sun beating down on it all day. I swam around a little, getting my body used to the water temp, dipping down and back up again, completely drenched. The water fell from my hair down my face. I glanced over as Molly dove down and back up, shaking her hair as she re-emerged. Her nipples were hard as rocks, poking through her bikini top, making it hard to take my eyes off of them. I don't know what she's doing to me suddenly, but I find it hard not to look away from her.

Molly swam over to the edge of the dock to grab her glass. She held herself up, sipping on the wine and looking over at me.

"You know." She begins. "I'm not oblivious."

"What do you mean?" I called out confused.

I watched her from the water as she tried to hide her smile.

"I love this song!" She said, ignoring me, as Porn Star Dancing, by My Darkest Days Ft. Zakk Wylde, comes on, blaring through the speaker.

She continues to do a dance, a little slutty, sexy dance, through the water as she begins to touch her body from her belly to her hair as she continues to hold the wine glass with the other hand.

"You're not oblivious to what?" I asked again, confused.

She continues to dance and ignores me. She focused on the song and continued to move her hand around her body. I kept my distance in the water, just watching.

"You ever been skinny dipping?" She asks, still ignoring my question.

"No. I haven't," I answered.

"You should give it a try." She replied. "It's so freeing.

"Yeah. Maybe. Some day." I smirk at the thought.

Molly continued to ignore me, and as the song continued, she set her wine glass down as she continued to rub her other hand up and down her body. As I watched, I then noticed her take her bikini top off and throw it behind her on the deck.

Woah! What are you doing?" I asked, as my eyes became huge, along with something else.

I saw Molly give a laugh, once again ignoring my inquiry. She's starting to piss me off with how much she's ignoring me. I drew a small grin as she started to dance and shimmy off her bottoms. She then dove under the water and disappeared for a minute.

"I feel so free!" She exclaims behind me.

I turned in the water, seeing that she was now behind me, staring at me with her cute little grin.

"What are you doing?" I asked.

"Come on, chicken." She said teasingly as she tossed her bottoms over my head, barely landing on the dock.

"Someday," I respond, still grinning.

"I promise you, you'll feel so free. So relaxed."

"I'm fine," I protested.

She swam near me and grabbed hold of my shoulders. Without any warning, she slid her hands from my shoulders to my waist. I started to back away.

"I'm just trying to help you be free!" She protests.

I chuckled as I swam towards the dock. It was my turn to mess with her. I grabbed my wine glass and took a sip. I grabbed my phone and skipped what was currently playing to *Bad Girlfriend* by Theory of a Deadman. I chuckled at my song choice as I took another sip of wine. I looked over to her and saw her give me an evil grin and a side-eye, seeming to realize my song choice.

"Fitting, isn't it?" I asked myself.

All Molly did was laugh, sing and dance through the water, still staring at me.

"Oh, come on already." She spoke. "I know you watched me change through the crack of the door in the hallway."

"I don't know what you're talking about," I answered, frozen.

"It's okay." She replied. "I saw you too, when your door was wide open, probably on purpose."

"You're mistaken." I continued to lie.

"I saw how big you are and how free you felt to let it all hang out. We're human. Must live life in the moment when it presents itself." She says almost shyly but still deviously.

"I...I...I didn't mean to," I stammered.

"Oh, stop lying." She said sternly.

Jekyll and Hyde, by Five Finger Death Punch, came on over the speaker behind me, and I lost all control. The lies left my mind, and the truth, well, the truth about her took over. The same feeling of red and anger poured out of me as I started to feel different once again. I looked down at the reflection in the water, and it wasn't mine staring back at me. It was the older, salt-n-pepper-looking man staring back at me. Along with the anger and violence. Confidence coursed through my body. I was fully erect at this point, without a care in the world.

"Fine." I exclaimed confidently and threw off my swim trunks behind me on the dock. I swam towards Molly and stopped inches from her. "Are you happy now?"

"Are you?" She asks, laughing.

"This is what you wanted," I replied, still cold and confident.

"Just trying to get you everything you've been looking for."
She replies gingerly.

I inched even closer, grabbing her in my arms, pressing myself onto her. We swam there for a minute, not saying anything, as her breasts touched my bare skin and my erection poked at her midsection. I moved my lips to her neck kissing it slowly and softly.

"That was a fast change of heart," she said, shocked.

"Shh...." I whispered, still kissing her neck. Moving my hand all over her body.

Molly gave out a whimper as she enjoyed herself, wanting more. I moved my hand underwater to touch her midsection, slowly going lower and teasing her.

"Not in the lake." I whispered in her ear.

"What do you have in mind?" she asked in a whisper.

"Follow me." I replied, still in her ear.

I headed towards the dock, looking behind me to have her follow. I hopped out of the lake, using my hands to boost me up onto the dock. I sat up on the ledge and moved my legs to stand up. I looked down, seeing Molly stare at my erection. She gave off a sexy grin as she moved closer to the dock's ledge.

I watched as she jumped up, using the edge of the dock as support, as her breasts bounced up and down. Her nipples were still hard as rocks, as she hoisted herself up. I'm still watching her move as I'm admiring her body.

She hopped up, spinning her legs around to stand up on her feet, her ass spread wide open for a moment, the full view of her perfect, toned buttocks. I licked my lips as I continued to admire the perfection in front of me.

"So. Where do we go now?" She asks as she moves closer to me, putting her hand on my chest.

"You'll see," I respond. "You'll just have to trust me."

I leaned down, grabbing her toned ass in my hands, as I gave her one more kiss on her neck. I then moved towards the lake shed, taking out my keys.

"You have keys to this?" She asks, giggling, still drunk from all the wine.

"Apparently my dad had a set; I found out the other day." I replied, trying to play it smoothly. "There's a table in here we can use."

"Kinky." She replied, interested.

I managed to keep her entertained as I unlocked the shed.

"I want to try something." I said as we entered. "Something Julie never lets me do."

"What's that?" she asked curiously.

"I want you to get up on that table, and I want to strap you down," I said sternly.

"Oh, you are kinky," She said surprisingly. "Okay, I'm down."

Molly sat up at the table and lay down. As she lay down, I fastened the straps over her hands and feet and just stared at her with a smirk.

Chapter Thirteen:

"Well, this is kinky," Molly said, smiling.

I moved around the table, staring down at her naked body. Her blonde hair lay messily behind her head. Her crystal blue eyes twinkled with excitement, watching me walk around the table. Her tiny nipples are harder than rocks, from the coldness coming from the steel table. I watched as she moved her legs back and forth, baring her clean-shaved goods. I continued to move around the table, staring and watching, not saying a word.

"So, what's the holdup?" She asks, staring at me. "Take a picture. It'll last longer."

"Ok," I said coldly.

I moved over to the table, where the camera was and picked it up. I headed back to the table and stood in front of her.

"Hey!" Molly exclaimed. "I was just kidding!"

"Relax," I said, still coldly. "No one will see this. Besides me, of course."

"You promise?" She asks.

"Trust me," I replied sternly. "I don't want Julie or John to ever see this."

"Okay." She said shyly.

As I stood in front of her, I snapped a picture of her, seeing her give off a shy grin. I walked behind her to stand behind her head and snapped another picture. I then set the camera down to the side for now. The voice in my head reminding me, "Take your time on the next victim."

I moved over to the table against the wall and grabbed a blindfold. I took the blindfold with me as I headed back over to Molly.

"What's that for?" she asked.

"Thought you were up for some fun," I said sternly.

"Never done something like this before." She chuckled. "But fuck it. We came this far."

Without saying anything, I put the blindfold on her eyes and tied it tightly.

"Can you see anything?" I asked, looking at her.

"No." She responded with a giggle.

"Good." I said as I moved over to where the stainless tools are kept.

I reached down, moving my hands over the cool, smooth tools, finally grabbing a short blade. I took the blade and held it in my hand, squeezing. Loving the feel course through my hand and through my body. I moved towards the table where Molly was lying, not moving. She was still blind, and most likely curious as to what I was going to do next.

I moved the tip of the blade over her body, starting with her throat, moving downward through her breasts, and down to her torso. I saw as she squirmed. Her nipples are getting harder.

"That tickled!" She exclaimed, laughing.

I watched her squirm around as the blade was tickling her. This was doing nothing for me. The way she was enjoying this made my erection go away. I was getting nothing. I felt nothing from this at all. I only felt anger. I was getting even more upset by her not feeling any pain yet, so I decided to take it up a notch.

Knowing that she couldn't see but still had the ability to speak was bothering me. After the last victim, the screaming was a bit loud, even though there was no one around; I didn't want to risk anything. I went over to the table with supplies and grabbed the duct tape. As I grabbed the duct tape, I took a piece from its roll. She must have heard what I was doing, because she asked, "What was that?" I ignored her stupid little question and put the piece over her mouth, hearing the muffled sounds escaping. Finally, as I put the tape over her mouth, I felt something course through my body.

I grabbed the knife again and ran it over her body once more. I haven't even kissed her body since she lay on the table. The only thing I thought about was how much of a stupid bitch she was for being so gullible. The way she looked had nothing to do with how it made me feel; it's how helpless she is and what I'm about to do to her body that gets me going.

I remembered from the last victim what happened when they felt too much pain, so I skipped the lidocaine this time and made sure I had some smelling salts at the ready for when she passed out.

I picked the knife back up and once again went up and down her body. Her nipples were still rock hard, pointing straight out for attention. I heard a whimper escape the duct tape as she was still clueless about what was about to happen.

She might be enjoying herself at this moment, but it was time to turn it up and finally have me feel something. I made an incision by her torso, leaving a small trail of blood trickling down. The whimper turned into a shocked scream as I made another incision on the other side of her torso.

I moved to take her blindfold off. I loved it when they watched me work. I untied the blindfold and saw her eyes go wide, filled with fear. No longer excitement.

The look she gave me finally brought back my erection. The sound of muffled pain and the sight of blood got me hot and bothered. She stared at me, eyes bugging out, as I adjusted myself in my boxers.

Before I continued, I let the two incisions soak in, as I moved to throw on the lab coat that was hanging on a hook in the corner. I wanted to make sure any blood splatter stayed in one spot and didn't ruin my clothes. I would be a walking forensic goody bag if I weren't careful.

I almost want to hear all the screams of pain and misery, but I'll take the tape off closer to the ending. Now that I had the coat on, I picked up the knife once more and made erratic incisions across her body. Some of the cuts were small; others were larger. The muffled screams continued, along with the tears running down her face.

I got bored with the knife and thought it was time for a little physical violence. I started by smacking her face. Boy did that feel great! Then I threw some punches at her all over in a rapid sequence. I even grabbed her throat and squeezed until I couldn't any longer. Her pretty little blue eyes turned red from the lack of oxygen to her brain.

I stopped for a minute to admire my work. I wasn't quite satisfied with the amount of torture I gave her. The voice in my head gave me an idea: "Use the drill," it spoke. I gave it a once-over. It was something I hadn't used in a while. In agreement with the voice in my head, or with myself, I really had no idea at this point. I moved over to the shelving hanging on the wall and grabbed the drill.

Once I had the drill, I brought it over to the table. I started drilling holes in random spots all over her body. I left multiple holes all over her body. All in spots that wouldn't kill her right away. That would ruin the fun, and the suffering needed to go on for a little while longer. The pain that escaped her was stronger than ever. Tears ran down from her bloodshot eyes. Her eyes were so wide with fear of what could be next and the pain of what had already happened. To my astonishment, she hasn't passed out yet. I had no idea how much of a fighter she truly was. I knew it was only a matter of time till she was about to pass out though.

As she continued to fight, I got bored with the drill. I stood there staring at all the cuts and drill holes all over her body and watched the blood leave her body. I thought now was a good spot to snap a picture of the work I've created.

I took the camera and stood at the end of the table, snapping some pictures. I did some close-ups of my work, along with some far shots. Muffled crying and small screams are all I heard from Molly. I decided to turn the intensity up even more. I'm still in shock because she hasn't passed out yet.

I went back to the wall of tools and instruments after setting the drill down in the cleaning pan. A pan I had designated for cleaning and sterilizing for my next victim. I studied the wall, looking for my next toy of torture. I stood there for a minute studying the tools in front of me. The voice in my head told me, "Yes, that cleaver looks fun." I shook my head in agreement.

I reached up and grabbed the cleaver from the wall. I walked back over to Molly and stared at her. Once she saw the cleaver in my hand, her eyes damn near bugged out of her head. I let out a diabolical laugh and raised the cleaver. I swung the cleaver down on her left hand and completely severed it.

The hand fell off to the side of the table as blood squirted out the empty hole. I was fully erect once again, letting out a slight laugh with a matching evil grin. The sound of muffled screams came out behind the duct tape. After a few moments,

Molly finally passed out from the pain. Luckily for me, I had the smelling salts next to me, ready for use.

Chapter Fourteen:

I continued to look down at Molly, lying there passed out from the pain. Her wild blonde hair wet from the sweat she produced trying to set herself free from the table. Her tight, toned body was covered in cut marks, drill holes and bruises had already started to form all over.

I looked down and stared at her hand that rested on the floor. I needed to cauterize the bleeding before she bled out from this. That would ruin the fun, and I was just getting started. I contemplated waking her up for the part of me cauterizing the wound, but she would probably pass out quickly. That would piss me off, and I would probably rush to the grand finale.

It was the hardest decision I had to make, but ultimately, I leaned towards keeping her passed-out option. For now, anyways, she was starting to lose a ton of blood, so I had to act quickly if I wanted to continue to have more fun.

I quickly went over to the table by the wall and grabbed a torch. I then grabbed a stainless-steel handle that had a circular curve at the end. I lit the torch and held the circular tool with the other hand, making it nice and hot. I held the torch to the tool as I walked back over to Molly. As the tool became bright red, I knew it was ready to begin the singe stage.

I moved the tool towards the hole in her arm, where the hand once was. As I held the tool to the empty hole, I turned the torch off and set it down. The smell of burning flesh filled the air, mixed with any hair that remained on the arm near where the wrist is. The remaining skin had melted around what remaining flesh was there, stopping the blood flow coming out. The colors surrounding the open flesh were a mixture of purplish-pink and black. The black color gave off a crisp texture.

I set the tool down since it did its job and picked up the camera. I took some shots of the brutal cut job and some more of all the other torture marks. After taking a few pictures, I set the camera back down to pick up the smelling salt. I popped one open as I placed it under her nose. Molly jerked awake quickly, giving off a loud gasp as she came to. She struggled to catch her breath.

Instantly, she started to sob again as she moved her head, looking around. The sobs began faster and harder. Her eyes filled fast with tears. She started to hyperventilate and tried to let out screams, but they were muffled behind the duct tape. Her eyes grew wide as she noticed her hand was gone, and she instantly became hysterical. The smell of burning flesh still hung in the air around us.

"Are you having fun yet?" I asked, laughing, as I watched her helplessly fight and cry uncontrollably.

The sounds of her pain and fear filled my every need, coursing through my body. The feeling fueling my need for more.

"If you're not having fun yet, wait for my next trick." I said, still laughing manically.

I moved back to the table at the back of the room to grab the stainless steel ball-peen hammer. The familiar feel of the coldness ran through my hands feeling great and powerful as I held it tightly. I gave off a cynical smile as I walked back to Molly.

I stood over her looking at her fight for her life as she continued to cry and scream in fear.

"Why? Why are you doing this?" She asked, the sound muffled through the duct tape. "Mike. Why?"

"Mike?" I asked, still staring at her. "Oh, that weak little boy? He's not here now."

"Wha...What?" Her cry muffled.

I just continued to laugh and smirk at her as I raised the hammer. I struck down on some of her joints, starting with her kneecaps, hearing the bones crunch. I swung multiple times, repeatedly, all at different areas on her body.

At this point, her body was mangled. She didn't even look like herself anymore. She was filled with holes and cuts, broken joints, and a missing hand and beaten with a ton of fresh bruises forming.

As Molly lay there torn apart, she looked defeated. She was no longer trying to scream. She was no longer trying to move around to attempt to escape. The only sounds coming from her were soft sobs and little moans of agony. I've reached the point of torture where it was becoming stale.

Once the victim either faced the reality of an ultimate demise or the fact that their mind gave up on their body and soul, it was no longer stimulating. It was time to finish. Almost sad. I had fun with Molly, but like the others, the end finally came.

I let out a sigh of disappointment but also a feeling of being impressed that she lasted longer than the others. I moved towards the table in the back to grab my last instrument of destruction. I grabbed the stainless hatchet in my hand, and with the other, I carefully felt the blade to feel its sharpness. The hatchet felt a little dull, so I had to sharpen it.

I turned on my sharpener as I moved the blade back and forth slowly and patiently. After a few moments of moving the blade around, I grabbed a cloth and wiped the blade. I could feel the sharpness through the rag and let out a grin. I was pleased with the feeling.

I moved back towards Molly and stared down at her, admiring my work one last time before I called it quits and struck the final blow. I raised the hatchet above my head, aiming for her throat.

"Thank you." I said through a laugh. "I had fun."

I struck down fast and hard, and with one swift motion, her head was severed from her body. I heard a soft thud as her head fell into the pan below the table. Blood started spraying out from the empty hole.

I set the hatchet down with the other tools that will need to be cleaned and, once again, picked up the camera. I took a final picture of Molly, this time with her head missing. My work was done. I gathered all the photos I took and wrote her initials on the back to be filed away in the correct place.

I went outside. Carefully looking around before I fully left the doorway to make sure I was still alone. I was there for a while as I noticed the sun started to set. I needed to gather up Molly's belongings before I could head back to the cabin.

I made my way over to the table to find her purse. As I made my way over, I could still hear my phone on the speaker playing music. *Scream for me* by One Bad Son was playing. I turned off the speaker, grabbed all our stuff and headed back to the shed.

Once inside, I searched through the purse to find her wallet. Once I found her wallet, I looked for her I.D. I took the I.D. out and placed it in the correct file in the cabinet.

As I shut the cabinet, I felt my pocket buzz. I reached my hand down and took my phone out of my pocket. I saw the screen light up with Julie's name on it.

"Shit." I said, looking at the screen, noticing that I had a few missed calls. "Hello?"

"When are you guys coming back? Dinner is almost ready!" Julie expressed.

"I'm about to head back," I answered. "I just finished gathering up my stuff."

"And Molly?" she asked.

"She said that she's enjoying herself and wants to stay a bit longer, and that she'll catch up," I said, lying.

"You think that's smart, leaving her?" Julie asked worriedly.

"No," I replied. "But you know how she is."

"Well, tell her to not be too much longer. It's going to be dark real soon." She spoke.

"I will," I assured her. "I'll see you soon."

As I hung up the phone, everything went dark once again, and before I knew it, I was staring at the door of the cabin.

Chapter Fifteen:

I stopped in my tracks and stared at the door to the cabin.

"God damnit." I whisper-yelled to myself.

My eyes felt heavy, and my head pounded. I rubbed my eyes, trying to get back to reality. I hate that this keeps happening. One moment I'm at the lake; the next, I'm standing right here. The worst part about it was the images came to me as soon as I fell asleep. When I'm dreaming, the truth comes out from what I did during the time I can't remember. Until then, everything is a blur, like living in a false reality. Everything clouded behind a cloud of haze.

I shook my head and blinked hard a few times before I headed up the stairs to the cabin. As soon as I opened the door a waft of the dinner Julie was making in the kitchen filled my nostrils. The scent made me forget everything that happened or didn't happen. The hell if I know.

The scent of a mixture of herbs seeped through my senses. Oregano, basil, parsley, and rosemary illuminated my nostrils. The smell of the roasted tomatoes, from what I assume was marinara, was heavenly. There was also a hint of garlic in the air.

I moved towards the kitchen. As I walked through the doorway, I saw Julie skipping around setting the table. She placed bowls, plates, glasses, knives and forks onto the tabletop. She aligned them neatly and perfectly.

"Hey you!" She said as she glanced up.

"Hey babe," I replied. "Anything I can do?"

"Um, could you open up a bottle of wine?" she answered me, still messing with the place settings. "That way it'll give it a bit to breathe."

"I think I can do that." I replied with a laugh.

"Hey guys." John said entering the room. "Smells amazing Julie. Where's Molly?"

"Thank you." Julie responded.

"Um, she wasn't ready to head back yet." I lied, still not remembering anything.

"What?" John said, concerned. "She knows it's getting late."

"You did tell her not to take much longer, right?" Julie looked at me.

"Yeah, I did." I replied to Julie, then turned to John. "Don't worry bud, she's going to be fine. The lake isn't far away."

"Well, I'm starving." He said hungrily.

"Is it proper to start without her?" Julie asked.

"Well, she knew you were making dinner, and she didn't leave with Mike, so that's on her," John replied. "let's eat."

"Okay, fine." Julie said as she made her way over to the oven.

She reached down and grabbed the sheet tray out of the oven and brought it over to the table. She took the tongs with one hand and set down the chicken parm on our three plates.

The chicken looked and smelled heavenly. The look of the golden-brown breading with the mozzarella cheese oozing on top of it made my mouth water. After she placed the chicken on our plates, she went back to the stove, set the pan down, and picked up a pot that was next to it. She brought over the pot and tonged some pasta onto our plates next to the parms. Fettuccini alfredo. Oh man, the pasta gleamed with the white sauce. As the steam from the pasta filled the air in front of us, the smell of Parmesan cheese and garlic heightened my senses.

"Holy shit." I said, looking at the food then up at her. "Babe, I didn't know you could cook like this."

"Thank you." She chuckled shyly.

"Looks amazing Julie." John said in agreement.

She went back to the stove to set the pot down and went over to the counter, grabbing a bowl. She placed the bowl down in the middle of the table.

"There's the salad, if y'all want any." She said, staring at us. "Now, pass the wine. My work is done."

We all started to eat, as my mouth continued to water. Julie filled her glass with the wine and passed the bottle around. We were all too busy filling our mouths with food and wine. We didn't really talk much. After a little while of stuffing our faces, all our looks seemed the same. Our plates were empty, and our stomachs were full.

"Man, oh man." John said, leaning back in his chair. "That was a hell of a meal."

"That was perfect babe." I said in agreement.

"Thank you." She replied smiling. Giving off a little blush. "Who's got dishes?"

"I got them." John answered.

"You sure?" I asked him. "You want help?"

"Nah, I'm good." He assured. I'm going to wait around for Molly."

"Okay." I spoke. "You want to head upstairs?" I asked Julie, turning towards her.

"Sure." She said, grinning.

I followed Julie up the stairs. I watched as her buttocks moved left and right. We haven't had quality time together in a while. I thought we would be all over each other since we got here, but I was wrong. I guess that would be my fault, being so distant and preoccupied with whatever the hell was happening to me.

As we entered our room, Julie went over to the nightstand and lit a couple of candles. As she lit the candles, I dimmed the lights. The room was setting the mood. We came together and I held her in my arms. Her head rested on my chest and my hand rubbed across her back, the other running through her hair.

As we stood there, our hearts started to pound against each other. The tension and passion of a long overdue connection filled our bodies, like a current through a wire. Our breaths started out slowly but started to grow faster and heavier as we stood there holding each other. She had goosebumps that appeared on her body, and I kissed the ones that were on her neck.

She moved her hands around my neck as I continued to kiss hers.

"You mean the world to me." I whispered in her ear.

"I love you so much." She whispered back.

I moved away from her neck and looked into her eyes; they were glistening with the wave from the candle. We held each other's gaze, our mouths centimeters apart from each other. She grabbed my shirt by my chest and pulled me all the way in. We stood there for a minute kissing each other's lips. The taste of her mouth was sweet, and I couldn't get enough of it.

We stood there kissing slowly and passionately until her hand touched my back under my shirt. We gradually sped up our kissing, still savoring our lust and chemistry with one another. She grabbed the bottom of my shirt as she pulled it over my head. As she took my shirt off, she threw it on the floor behind me, and I moved to take her shirt off in return. Her shirt fell to the floor, leaving her in her red bra.

We continued the passionate kissing, as I took one hand to unfasten her bra, moving the other one to grab her ass. I managed to undo her bra, dropping it on top of her shirt, then joined my other hand, grabbing handfuls of her ass, squeezing them on and off. Our kissing became stronger and less controlled. She reached for my shorts to pull them off.

My trunks fell down my legs, and I took turns with each one of my legs, stepping out of them. I then kicked them to the side. I slowly moved my hands around her waist and slid her shorts off as she kicked them off. My hands went right back to her buttocks, squeezing both cheeks, staring at her matching red thong. I kissed one nipple, then the other, teasing them with my tongue as they got harder by the second. Julie let out a little quiet whimper.

Julie moved her hand from my chest down to my groin. My erection getting longer and harder each time she moved down. She grabbed the band of my boxers and pulled them down. She continued to work her hands in my groin area, turning me on even more. She kissed my neck, then my chest. I put my fingers under the band of her thong and pulled them off as I moved my groin into her.

With all our clothes finally off, our chemistry shot off like fireworks. She threw me on the bed and climbed on top, straddling me. She kissed my neck, right below my ear, as I moved my hands down her back to her ass, squeezing and spreading. We both let out moans and groans as we lost control, letting the lust completely take over.

After a little while, being lost in our lust and erotic behavior, we lay on our sides of the bed. Her head rested on my chest as she was sound asleep. I stared up at the ceiling, almost out of breath. I was reliving the intimacy that we just shared. Man, did I miss how powerful our chemistry was. I needed to take a piss, so I carefully got up, making sure not to wake her. I sat up in bed and headed towards our bathroom.

I went to the toilet, lifted the seat and pissed. It seemed like the longest piss of my life. When I finished, I closed the lid back down and flushed the toilet. I moved to the sink to wash my hands. As I washed my hands, I stared at myself in the mirror, giving myself a celebratory look. I looked away and splashed some water on my face. When I looked back in the mirror, I damn near let out a small shriek.

The salt-n-pepper-haired man stared back at me once again. This shit has got to stop.

"What do you want from me?" I asked my reflection, or the salt-n-pepper man in the mirror.

"Revenge." It spoke.

"For what?" I asked, confused. "Who are you?"

"Come now." It replied. "You know exactly why and who I am."

'I don't! I don't know why you keep appearing!" I exclaimed.

"I'm Dr. Underwood." The reflection said cold and calmly. "I know; you know all about me."

"This isn't real. This can't be happening." I said shakily.

"You were an easy target." The doctor began. "Your mind and soul were easy to control."

"Stop." I said, shaking my head. "Stop it right now and get out of my head."

"You're weak!" The doctor continued. "And we're not done having fun."

"I'm not weak!" I protested. "You can't control me!"

"I have, and I'm about to take complete control." The doctor assured me sternly. "I was having fun with you. Toying with your mind, now I'm bored and I'm going to finish what I started."

"No!" I cried out.

"Goodbye, Michael." The doctor finally said.

I reached for the faucet handle and turned the water off. I grabbed a rag that was hanging nearby and cleaned up the water mess around the sink. When I was done, I hung the rag back up where it was hanging, neatly. I glanced back in the mirror at my reflection as I laughed uncontrollably, running my hands through my salt-n-pepper hair.

I turned the light off in the bathroom and entered the bedroom. I sat down on the bed, about to lie back down.

"What were you laughing at?" Julie asked sleepily, rubbing her eyes.

"Nothing." I said coldly. "Go back to sleep; I'll see you in the morning."

Chapter Sixteen:

I watched Julie lay back down and instantly fell back to sleep. I smirked at how comfortable She looked, while thinking about the pain that's easily accessible, teasing me to grab it and squeeze till her last breath left her body. I gave her one last glance, staring at her full naked body as her chest rose up and down slowly, taking her sweet breaths, sound asleep.

I turned away from temptation and opened the bedroom door to leave. I closed the door quietly and started down the hall pausing at John and Molly's room. I reached for their door handle and carefully cracked the door open just enough to peek inside.

I glanced at the mirror in the corner of the room, the same mirror I used to look at Molly the other night. The image of her hard body still fresh in the memory. Her toned ass and hard nipples left an impression in my mind. Those images then became flooded with the sight of the torture marks she shortly endured after that. The only thing I see in the mirror now is the sight of John asleep in bed alone.

"I wonder when he gave up the search for Molly?" I asked myself with an evil grin.

I closed the door quietly as the satisfaction of everyone asleep coursed through me. How sweet it is knowing they're vulnerable now in case I wanted to do anything right this second! I continued down the hall and headed down the stairs towards the den area of the cabin.

Off to the side, there was a mini bar cart set up with fancy rock glasses and expensive-looking carafes filled with brandy and scotch. As I approached the cart, I grabbed one of the glasses, reached in the ice bin for some Ice and dropped it into the glass. I then grabbed the carafe that contained the scotch as I breathed in its strong odor. I poured myself a drink and took a sip, enjoying the burn as it slid down my throat.

As I stood there taking slow sips of scotch, I started to contemplate my next moves. I wanted to toy with John and Julie a little longer, so they were out of the equation for now. The only other target would be Frank. It was time to seek my revenge, now that I've found my way to get to him. Frank trusts Mike, and I fully plan to use him to get my hands on Frank finally. I've been waiting for the longest time to make my move. I thought about the course of action for a few moments as I continued to take slow sips of the scotch. The burn from the liquor crept its way down to my stomach, and I was starting to feel great and calm. I noticed a small chest off in the corner of the room, close by the mini-bar cart. I approached it and examined its beauty.

The small chest was indeed beautiful. I find myself appreciative of art, as it's probably the most humane thing left to me. The chest had these designs on it that put me in a trance. It was fully made of wood, but it was painted with bronze, red and a little bit of a yellow tint. The designs on them remind me of walking around in New Orleans; you'll know exactly what I'm talking about. The design was loud with its color and design. It would make you stop and appreciate the energy coming off the chest, or maybe it's just the scotch that's making me feel this way as I take another drink of the liquor.

As I stopped paying attention to the chest's beauty, I went to open it. Of course it was locked, as expected. I grabbed the set of keys that was in my pocket. I fiddled with the set on the ring and grabbed the smallest one first. I then inserted the small key into the keyhole on the chest. It was the only spot that was gold. The key fit perfectly, as I turned the key and unlocked the chest. As I lifted the lid, I saw the most beautiful gun lying right before me, resting inside the chest.

The gun, to my knowledge, was a beautiful Colt Python. Guns typically weren't my cup of tea, but I did enjoy a good-looking weapon. This revolver was simple. It had a stainless-steel barrel with a brownish, bronze handle. From what I know, the barrel contains a nickel finish to it. The revolver was kept in great condition, and it was well polished. The polish gave it a nice, shiny appearance. I also know that there are two different sizes. There's a six- and a four-inch Python, and this one looks larger than a four-inch. It gave off a frightening look. It's perfect for what I want to use it for: intimidation and maybe a little fun. I mean why not since it's right here in front of me, right?

The one aspect of the weapon that I am aware of is the ability to have a double-action chamber. Oh man, this weapon could do some damage. This gun just gave me a half-chub, just thinking about the kind of pain and damage it could do in such a short time.

I grabbed the revolver in my hand and immediately felt its power. Next to the Python, in the chest, were some bullets lying in a perfect row. The .357 bullets were shiny and caught your attention. The thought smacked me in the face: this gun is a trophy weapon that was never supposed to be used. Such a fucking waste. If that was truly the case, then it should be in a display case and not hidden away inside this beautiful chest.

I loaded the chamber of the Python and carefully closed the lid to the chest. I wish that Frank were at his shop right now, but unfortunately, I would have to wait until the store opens tomorrow morning. Now that I know Frank never has anyone that ever goes in there for his stupid shit he's collected over the years, that's not going to be the hard part. The hard part is figuring out how I'm going to sneak away again.

I finished my drink, tucked away the gun and headed up the stairs, back to the bedroom. As I reached the room, I stashed the gun in the nightstand on my side of the bed and looked over at Julie, still sound asleep the way I left her. When the gun was stashed and hidden, I climbed in the bed and lay down, anxious for the next morning.

Chapter Seventeen:

I woke up from the short sleep I've had and stretched as I sat up at the end of the bed. I quickly threw on some clothes that were lying around and rushed out of the bedroom. I made my way down the stairs and towards the kitchen. As I entered, I saw both Julie and John lingering.

As Julie noticed I entered, she asked if I wanted some coffee. I nodded my head in agreement as I moved closer to John.

"You have any luck finding Molly?" I asked, trying to hide my smirk.

"No." He replied, shaking his head. "I stayed out as long as I could searching for her but headed back to the cabin as it was getting later."

"Damn." I said, faking the sincerity.

"I was really hoping she would have come back by the time I got up this morning, but she's still not here." John said concerningly.

"Maybe we can split up and look for her now that we have daylight." I said, trying to sound supportive.

Julie handed me the cup of coffee as she shook her head in agreement. "Anything to find out where she's been."

"Well, we better get a move on." I spoke.

As we all agreed to go our separate ways to search for Molly, I thought it was a perfect time to pay Frank a visit. I poured my coffee into the cup, since there was no point wasting a good cup. John and Julie already left, as I made my way back to the bedroom. I climbed the stairs and headed straight to the room. Once I got to the room, I made my way to the nightstand to grab the revolver that I hid away earlier. I reached down and loaded the chamber and placed it behind my back, using the belt to keep it in place, and then pulled my shirt down over it.

As I left the bedroom, I thought to myself how easy this would be, knowing Frank has a lot of trust in Mike. All I would have to do is act like Mike to get myself inside with him. I made my way back down the stairs, headed towards the door where our shoes were and slipped on a pair. After I had my shoes on, I opened the door and walked outside. The weather was perfect, yet again. It was about 75 degrees with a few clouds in the sky and a nice slight breeze. The sun was applying the much-needed heat to counterbalance the cool breeze.

I made my way down the long drive and headed to Frank's store. I can almost feel the rush of excitement and anticipation through my veins. The closer I got to the shop, the more satisfied I felt.

Chapter Eighteen:

I finally approached Frank's shop and opened the door. I walked in and noticed Frank standing behind the counter organizing his useless shit. As I reached the counter, he finally noticed me.

"Mike." He said as he drew a cough. "You looking for a job?"

"No." I replied, forcing a little laugh.

"Well, what is it this time?" He asked. "Can't be that you like me this much."

"I just have something on my mind that I would like to run by you." I replied with a lie.

"Well, alright." He said, continuing to cough. "Give me a few minutes to get myself situated, and I'll meet you in the back room."

"Okay." I said as I started to walk over to the room.

"Brew up some coffee." Frank called out as I almost made it to the room.

I entered the backroom and glanced around. Even though I've been back here before, it still looks like shit. I can't get over the difference between the back of the store and the front. The front is neat, clean and organized, while back here it's messy, dusty, and unorganized.

I headed over to where the coffee pot was and started fixing up a pot. I grabbed a filter, inserted it into the holder, took the pot over to the small sink that was back here, and filled the pot up with water. I dumped the water into the maker and reached for the container of coffee. I scooped out some coffee grounds into the filter, closed the lid and hit the power button.

"Man, all this stupid shit just to get Frank alone," I thought to myself.

I headed over to the small table that was in the middle of the room and took a seat, sipping on the coffee I brought with me.

A few moments passed by, and Frank finally came in. The coffee was still not ready, so he sat down across from me.

"So, what's on your mind?" He asks, staring at me.

"I've been having these dreams that seem so real. There are images that seem like I've encountered before, but I'm not sure if I have or not." I began.

I looked at Frank, and he's zoned in, listening to what I have to say.

"It's almost like I black out and then regain consciousness, as if it's a trippy little trip." I continued.

"I see." Frank said as he stood up to head over to the coffee pot. "Maybe it's just all the stories about the killer that you've heard recently creating these bad dreams."

"That's just it." I began as I stared at Frank's back as he poured himself a cup of coffee. "It's actually not a dream, but it's reality." I finished, pointing the gun at him and waiting for him to turn around.

As Frank turned around, finishing getting his cup of coffee together, he looked at me and then at the gun in my hands.

"Mike, what are you doing?" He asked with a sense of heightened fear.

"Mike isn't here anymore." I said coldly.

"What do you mean?" Frank asked, trembling a bit.

"It's me." I shot back. "Don't you recognize me?"

"Me who?" Frank looked confused.

"It's Jacob!" I exclaimed.

As I said the name, Frank dropped the cup of coffee onto the floor. The cup shatters into pieces, and the hot liquid goes everywhere.

"What do you mean?" He asked, still in a state of confusion.

"Mike's no longer here; I'm in control now." I spat. "He was an easy, weak target to take over his mind."

"You're telling me that you're Dr. Jacob Underwood?" Frank asked, trying to piece everything together.

"Wow, look here. We have a brilliant man over here." I said sarcastically. "I've been making Mike do everything I wanted him to."

"But how?" Frank asked.

"Well, the stories are true." I began. "As a doctor, I investigated all sorts of medical practices. That includes witchcraft. I remembered a certain curse during my studies and put a curse on the woods."

"How does all the other deaths add up then?" He asked with sweat starting to form on his brows.

I've used multiple individuals to do my bidding over the years, but they were all weak and useless." I began to explain. "Mike was the only one that was fit enough for the task but easy enough to weaken his mind."

"What do you want with me?" He asked, still trembling.

"Revenge," I replied coldly.

"For what?"

"You don't remember pointing a gun at me, chasing me into the woods?" I asked angrily.

"You were a madman!" Frank exclaimed. "And you still are!"

I gave out a cynical laugh and looked at the weakened man standing in front of me.

"Enough with the questions!" I blurted out. "I'm getting bored and I'm only looking for some fun."

"So, you're just going to shoot me then?" He asked, terrified.

"Oh, no," I chuckled. You're a special case."

"What do you mean by that?" He asked.

"I'm going to have fun with you." I spoke. "Going to take as much time as I can afford. I do have other things to get to soon."

I pointed the gun higher, ushering Frank to move over to the chair. He hesitantly walked over to one of the chairs very slowly and sat down. I kept the gun pointed at him and found some duct tape to secure him to the seat. Once I had his ankles and wrists secured to the chair, I stood in front of him.

"Now let's see what kind of nasty shit you have in here to use on you." I said, beginning to examine the room more closely.

Chapter Nineteen:

I started looking around to decide on my first toy to play with. I spotted a toolbox resting on a workbench, and my eyes lit up. I moved over to the table and opened the box. Oh man, there was plenty to use inside here. The feeling of excitement coursed strongly through my body.

Inside the box, there were a pair of pliers, screwdrivers, a small hammer and a bunch of nails. I'm about to have so much fun! I gathered the tools that I would start with and moved over to the table where Frank was sitting. I laid out the tools on the table. I put the hammer down, the pliers next to it, followed by the screwdriver and the nails. I stood up there for a moment, admiring the tools of torture and then Frank. His eyes were bugging out of his head looking at the tools in front of him. Sweat continued to fall down his face, and I could bet his heart was racing a mile a minute.

I reached down and picked up the pair of pliers but stopped dead in my tracks. I heard the bell ring above the front door and could see a tiny bit of relief coming from Frank. I moved quickly but quietly towards the door to the backroom and slowly closed the door. I looked at him and motioned with my finger to my lips in a shh position.

I stood still, with my ears perked listening intensely and patiently to whoever entered the store. Frank's eyes were darting around in fear back as they continued to bulge.

"Hello?" The customer called out. "Anyone here?"

Everything was silent in the backroom, anxiously waiting for them to leave.

"Hello?" The voice continued to call out, moving closer to the door in front of me.

I heard a knock on the door and raised the revolver to Frank's head. Everything remained silent.

"Anyone here?" The voice asked again. "The sign says you're open."

"Fuck." I mumbled under my breath.

After a few minutes and a few more knocks, I heard the bell above the front door once more. I waited a few more moments and moved towards the door. I slowly unlocked the door and carefully opened it. I peeked out of it and saw nothing. I slowly left the back room and cautiously looked around the store. I came up empty-handed, saw no one, and hurried to the front door. I turned the open sign around so it said "closed" and locked the door. Finally satisfied I made my way back to the back room, without taking the chance of being interrupted again I shut and locked this door as well.

When the store was finally locked up, I made my way back to Frank. I reached down and picked up the pair of pliers once more.

"I'm sorry about that." I said, trying to fake being apologetic. "Where were we?"

Frank started to hyperventilate and let out a muffled cry.

"Oh, there, there." I spoke. "We're about to start having fun."

I grabbed one of his hands and took one of his fingers with my other hand. I placed the plier on his fingernail and pulled at it away from his body. The whole fingernail was attached to the tip of the pliers, and blood started to gush from the open wound.

"Oh, baby!" I exclaimed. "Woo, that's exhilarating!"

Frank's breathing became faster, and tears started to pour from his eyes. I continued to pull apart his fingernails one at a time, laughing as I was doing it. His one hand was dripping blood from the open wounds as I set all the nails down on the table in front of him.

"See, we're having a blast!" I cried out, laughing uncontrollably. "Don't worry, I'll give you a minute before I start on the other hand."

The fear, tears, and blood were getting me overly excited. It almost sounds like a rock song that Mike listens to. The band's name could be **Destruction** or **The Torturer**. I chuckled at myself for my silly thoughts. Even my mind goes all over the place from time to time. I ripped off each fingernail quickly and with excessive force.

When I was done, he had blood coming out of both hands. All his fingernails were on the table in front of Frank.

"Hee- Hee." I chuckled. "This little piggy went to the market."

I sang the nursery rhyme as I played around with each nail. I slapped Frank a couple of times in the face as he appeared to be starting to doze off.

"Hey!" I shouted. "Pay attention before you piss me off!"

Frank's eyes opened wide once more when I shouted. Torturing men is a bit easier than torturing women. Women, especially if they're not trained, pass out from the pain quicker than men, or if the woman's tolerance isn't high enough to sustain the pain. On the other hand, torturing men becomes boring a lot quicker. Which is where I'm currently at. It was time to move on to the next tool.

The hammer looked great. It was calling me. Usually, I get excited to use the hammer. I would break a few bones, listening to its cracking noise. Ahh, such a relaxing sound to listen to. Unfortunately, this hammer is small and one would have to use excessive force to gain that satisfaction. It could even cause more damage than I'm willing to add now, since I want to inflict more damage after I've used the hammer. My imagination went straight to hammering the nails into Frank's body. Almost like acupuncture, except with nails. I laughed to myself at the thought and images.

I'm a doctor. I know all the right places to put all the nails and not do extreme damage. I picked up a nail and the hammer, ready to place the first strike. As Frank watched me, he squirmed in the chair frantically. His eyes are huge once again, knowing what is about to happen.

I inserted the first nail in Frank, followed by another. I started out slow at first, observing Frank flinch and squirm as each nail went through his body. I gradually grew faster with each nail until he had about a dozen all over him. I had one in each of his hands, pinning him to the chair. There was one in each knee, his thighs, and a few in each arm. There were some on his shoulders and chest area, away from the heart.

Blood pools started dripping down from each nail. He had blood spilling out in slow, small streams throughout his body and where I ripped his fingernails off. I eventually got bored with the hammer and nails, so I set the hammer back down on the table.

The next tool was the screwdriver. Man, that screwdriver was dirty. The head was all rusty and didn't look like it had been cleaned in years.

"Are you ready for this?" I asked, waving the screwdriver around by his face. He continued to squirm about, slower than before, due to the amount of pain he had endured. The muffled cries began louder through the duct tape.

I stood in front of him, admiring the work that I had done. I stared deep into his bulging eyes and gave an evil grin. I took the screwdriver and drove it into his thigh, close to the nail that was driven deep inside. A muffled howl came out of Frank, along with the sounds of anguish and pain. Tears continued to flow heavily, and you could tell he was getting weaker by the second. I'm shocked that he's still conscious. He's tougher than I thought. I loved that he was still coherent, making the torture remain enjoyable.

I took the screwdriver out of his thigh, watching the blood spurt out, and drove it into his other thigh. Frank's reaction was the same as before. The excitement continued to course through my body. I pulled the screwdriver back out and quickly jammed it into his left hand and then the right hand.

Frank was looking like a complete mess. Blood trickled everywhere. His tears hadn't stopped, and his breathing was shallow but quick under the duct tape.

I then thought to myself, how I wished I had a camera to capture my work of art. My camera should still be at the shed along with all my other goodies. An idea dawned on me.

"You got a camera in this dump Frank?" I asked, smiling.

Frank ignored my question, as he was too weak to bother with a muffled answer, and he was too busy crying and trying to calm his breathing. He was still looking around aimlessly. Fear and pain at an all-time high.

"Don't get up." I said through laughter. "I'll go check for myself."

As I headed to the front of the shop, I continued my hysterical laughter. I moved quickly up and down the rows, quickly scanning all the useless shit on its shelves. Row after row, useless shit after useless shit, I finally came across a few cameras resting on a shelf. I looked at each one, but only one caught my attention. It was like the one that's at the shed. A camera that can print a picture immediately after it's taken.

I picked the camera up and took it with me back to the room where Frank was still sitting. I stood in front of Frank with the camera pointed at him. I took pictures of all my work, including all the nails, his missing fingernails and the stab wounds. As the pictures came out of the camera after each shot, I set them on the table. Once they fully developed and became clear, I shoved them in Frank's face.

"Look!" I exclaimed. "Look at my art!"

Frank tried not to look, but once he did, he started to shake uncontrollably from crying and his quickened breaths. I set the pictures back down on the table. The feelings of anger and impulsion rushed through me. I quickly grabbed the screwdriver and drove it into Frank's body in rapid, consecutive motions. I stabbed him repeatedly. I moved faster, letting out all my rage.

"Ahhhhh!" I screamed.

At this point, Frank looked fucking awful. He was covered in blood, and his eyes were barely open. It was starting to look like the end of the road for him. Initially, I wanted to use the gun on him and just slowly blow him apart, but I absolutely hate using a gun on my victims. It's too quick. If I hadn't already done such a number on the old man, I would blow apart his joints and then end it. I feel as if even one gunshot wound would probably kill him instantly.

I think I'll settle by taking one of his knives from the front of the shop and cutting his throat wide open. I'll watch him bleed out as he struggles to take his final breath. I walked back to the front of the store and made my way behind the counter. I looked at the different types of knives till I finally made my choice. It was a long, skinny blade that seemed very sharp. The handle was golden with a silver line going down the middle. I was satisfied with my choice and once more returned to Frank.

As I stood in front of him, I reached for the duct tape to pull it off. At this point, he's not going to be able to scream or shout, since he's very weak. I slowly pulled back the tape and studied his reaction.

"Any last words?" I asked.

"I should have killed you when we had the chance." Frank managed to say through his short breaths.

"Yes." I agreed. "That was your mistake."

I stared deep into his eyes as I raised the knife to his throat. With a slow motion over his throat, I cut it from ear to ear. I kept my eyes on him as the blood rushed out and his gurgles started, trying to regain his last few breaths. After a moment passed, the gurgling stopped and the fight for air came to a cease. Frank was now dead, sitting in a pool of blood.

"How fun." I said out loud, staring at my finished work.

Chapter Twenty:

"What a fucking mess." I said, looking at the shit show in front of me.

I'll deal with this later, I thought to myself. For now, I'll just keep the shop locked up and gather up a few things. I got a new camera and a knife out of this whole ordeal. I grabbed a sheath to conceal the blade of the knife and hooked it to my side on the belt. I placed the revolver behind my back and pulled my shirt over it to keep it hidden. I grabbed the camera and the pictures from the table. I placed the pictures into my pocket and made my way to the front of the store.

After making sure the front looked untouched, I made sure the closed sign was still flipped the right way and locked the door behind me. I looked around, and there wasn't a soul in the area. At least no one would see me leaving. It was getting later in the day, about mid-afternoon. I was in that shop for a few hours. I hope John and Julie were still occupied trying to find Molly and not beginning to wonder where I took off to.

I decided to head over to the shed so I could put these pictures with all the other pictures. I headed in the direction of the lake. The temperature outside was at its peak for the day. It was about 75 degrees. The slight breeze felt nice as it made the leaves in the trees wave slowly. The breeze came when a cloud covered the sun, but once the clouds moved out of its way, the heat felt great on your skin.

I continued down the path surrounded by trees on both sides of me, not a soul around, until I got closer to the lake. It was John, sitting on the picnic table with his head in his hands.

"Hey John." I called out as I approached the table.

"Hey." He said warily, looking up.

"I take it no luck?" I replied, trying to give a shit. "Have you heard from Julie?"

"No. You?"

"That's a no for me again." I replied, faking sympathy. "Maybe she had better luck."

"I wanted to check in on that shed over there, but it's locked." He said, pointing at the nearby building. "And I can't look inside either. She could be in there."

"I was on my way over here for that reason." I lied. "I found out that I have a key to it, so I was going to open it and find out."

"Really?" His eyes lit up.

"Yeah." I looked at him hiding my smile. "You want to join me?"

"Hell yeah." He said excitedly.

We both headed over to the shed, and I took out my keys from my pocket. I slid the key into the hole and unlocked the door. I opened the door and gave an ushering motion to let him walk in first.

"Damnit." He exclaimed, looking around.

"Nothing?" I asked, as I followed behind him.

"No, but this place seems strange." He spoke.

"How so?" I asked as I reached for the revolver tucked in my back and pointed it at him.

"I mean, look at this place." He said, waving his hand around.

"I don't see anything wrong." I said with anticipation.

"What the fuck are you doing Mike?" He said as he turned to finally face me.

"I'm going to need you to shut the fuck up John." I said strongly.

"What's gotten into you man?" John asked.

"Get up on the table and shut the fuck up." I said once again.

"Dude, let's talk about this." He started to say.

"I'm not going to repeat myself John." I said, waving the revolver in a motion toward the table.

As I was motioning John to the table, he slowly and cautiously climbed onto the table. When he got on top of the table, I strapped him down tightly.

"Did you do something to Molly?" He asked.

"Ha, Ha." I just laughed at him as I finished the last strap.

"Mike!" He exclaimed. "Did you do something to Molly?"

"First." I said, slamming my hand down on the table. "I'm not Mike. He's no longer here."

"What the fuck are you talking about?" John asked, confused.

"Mike was weak, but just enough to do what I needed him to do." I begin to explain.

"You having a psych break or something?" He asked.

"My name is Doctor Jacob Underwood." I stated, backhanding John across the face. "I took Mike's mind over. I control him now."

"This doesn't make any fucking sense." John proclaimed.

"I'll ask the fucking questions!" I screamed, slamming my hand down again.

John stared at me with a shocked expression, watching my every move. The look of confusion spread wide across his face.

"What did you do to Molly?" He asked concernedly.

"Damnit." I said, getting extremely pissed off.

I walked over to the back table and grabbed what looked like a pair of tongs and took out my knife. I then grabbed the torch to get the knife nice and hot. As soon as the knife turned a bright red, I turned off the torch and headed back over to John. I grabbed his face and held it tightly.

"Take your tongue out!" I demanded. "Or I'll fucking blow your head off right now."

John eventually did what I asked and stuck his tongue out for me. Once I saw the tongue, I took the tool and grabbed a hold of it. I held it securely and took the knife to cut his tongue out of his mouth. Once his tongue was detached, he started to squirm and breathe heavily. He had tears starting to form from the pain as blood started flowing out of his mouth. The cut was clean and fast.

"Now, you were asking about Molly?" I asked John, staring at the battered man in front of me. "I wouldn't worry yourself too much about her." John attempted to speak. His face indicated pent-up anger.

He was trying his damn best to say something. Most likely he was trying to tell me off.

"You're precious, little Molly was really into Mike." I explained. "I did you a favor."

His expression hasn't changed. His eyebrows were pinched together, and he was trying to force his hands free. He kept moving his hands and feet, expecting to bust free.

"She was all over Mike in the water." I continued. "That hard body was begging for Mike to touch it. Luckily for me, she was so fucking gullible. I was able to get her right on this table. She went so willingly, thinking I was about to give her the best lay of her pathetic life. She's quite the little slut."

Tears started to form in John's eyes as the new emotion started to overpower the emotion of hate.

"You really want to know what happened to Molly?" I asked, watching the changes of emotions on John's face. "I can show you exactly what I did to her."

I went to the back of the room to the filing cabinet to grab the pictures from the correct tab and brought them over to John.

"Look!" I exclaimed, waving the photos in front of his face. "Look at her beauty."

John looked at the pictures, then turned his head away, closing his eyes. The tears fell heavily as he closed his eyes once again.

"I did a number on her." I said, laughing. "A little work of art."

John continued to sob, shaking slightly.

"This one is my favorite." I said, pointing at the picture of Molly's head cut off. "I should have kept her head around so I could keep paying her a visit whenever I felt lonely."

John continued to cry uncontrollably.

"Okay, that's enough of you being such a fucking baby." I said through gritted teeth. "Now it's your turn to have some fun."

John continued to look away from me, shaking his head in disbelief.

"Oh, come on." I began. "Think about all the fun we're about to have."

I contemplated what I wanted to do to him first. I need to switch it up and do something different, but I'm not sure exactly what to do. I thought while I took a minute to figure it out, I could just cut him up a bit.

I walked over to the side table, closer to the window, and grabbed my bag of goodies. I brought it back to the table and opened it up, displaying the stainless steel of torture instruments. I glide my hand over the cool steel, feeling its potential power. As I moved my hand over the tools, I stopped when I reached the scalpel.

I slid the scalpel out from its resting spot and held it up, looking at its shine. I then looked at John and he glanced at it for a second, then looked away. Fear was lively in his eyes from the split second I stared into them.

I took the scalpel with one hand, and with the other I held his face tightly. I moved the scalpel over his face, watching the fear grow in his eyes. His eyes followed the blade as much as they could with me holding his face tightly. After I had enough of toying around, I finally made the first small incision. As I cut down his face, I watched the small stream of blood slide down his cheek to his chin.

I could hear the attempted sound of pain coming from him, but it was so faint and boring. I made another cut on the other side of his cheek, this one a bit longer than the first, yet again watching the trickle of blood fall slowly down his face. He now has two little streams of blood running down his face.

I felt a sense of excitement and boredom flow through me. I still don't know what to do next, and it is starting to piss me off. I took my rage and made slice marks all over his torso. John's reaction was much better than when I cut his face. The failed attempts to make a sound were funny to me. It all sounded garbled. Not coherent, just little groaning noises.

"Man, you sound like Frankenstein." I said, laughing uncontrollably. "Merrr, Grrrr, Gahhhh."

John looked down at his torso, looking at all the cut marks, along with all the blood flowing out of each incision.

"I'm sorry." I said, unapologetic. "Cat got your tongue?"

As I stood there laughing uncontrollably, I had a bunch of ideas run through my head. They all hit me at once.

"Oh man, John, I have a fun-filled evening for us. "I said contemplating the order I wanted to go with. "I just don't know where to start."

The thoughts swam around in my head, anxious to do them all. I just couldn't figure out the order to do them in.

"That's it!" I exclaimed. "I'm so excited!"

I reached down in my toolbag and pulled out a pair of pliers. As I set the pliers down on the table, I went to the back wall and grabbed a battery with jumper cables. I set those down next to the pliers. I'll start with these first, looking at the tools in front of me. I'll have another trick up my sleeve after this. I wanted to make sure I had the equipment at the ready.

I picked up the pliers and held John's head tightly with my other hand. I forced open his mouth and moved the pliers to his right molar. I started pulling and tugging, forcing his tooth out of his mouth. As I finally got the tooth free, blood came rushing out from his gums. John let out a garbled cry as he was still incoherent. Tears still flooded his eyes as he was sobbing uncontrollably. I loved every minute of his pain and anguish. The feelings of power and excitement rushed over me. I was having too much fun.

I waited a moment before I attempted to take another tooth. I spun around and around, singing and dancing. Not a fuck in the world. I'm savoring the moment of my brilliant mind, too excited. I must control my impulses. There's much to do, and I can't wait.

After a few minutes of twirling around, dancing and singing, I was ready for more.

"The dentist is ready for you." I said, laughing.

I went back to work, taking his head with one hand and pulling teeth with the other. I managed to yank five teeth out of his mouth. The teeth were lying on the table in a row. John had blood gushing out of his mouth. He was no longer loud with his cries and groans. Now he was quiet, still sobbing uncontrollably. I did a number on his mouth. His tongue is missing, and now there are gaps from the missing teeth.

"I should make a necklace with your teeth." I laughed, playing around with the teeth on the table.

John started to look weak, lying on the table. He didn't bother to squirm or make any noise. The look of defeat raced across his face. The fear in his eyes was minimal, and his sobs slowed down. I couldn't have this. I have more work left to do.

"I'm going to need you to wake up John." I said as I grabbed the jumper cables. "I've got something that might spark your attention."

I continued to laugh crazily as I reached for the cables. As the volts raced through John's body, he started shaking and twitching. His hands and legs were shaking so badly, I almost thought he was going to break out of the restraints. When his eyes started to roll in the back of his head, I stopped shocking him.

"I'll give you a minute, John boy." I said, watching him. "At least you won't bite your tongue."

The fear was starting to come back in his eyes, but I can see he was still weak and didn't show any sign of pain. This was getting ridiculous. I wanted to shock him once more, but that would just weaken him even more. I wanted to accomplish at least one more torture method. I was excited for this one. It was a hard decision to not continue with the shock "treatment." I should have started with that. If only he had shut his fucking mouth, I wouldn't have to cut his tongue out of his mouth.

I stepped back and shook my head, trying to clear my thoughts. My mind was swimming, starting to not make sense. I picked up the battery and cables and headed towards the back of the room. I set down everything on the back table and looked at the wall. For a moment I just stood there trying not to think about anything. Still trying to straighten my thoughts out. My eyes scanned the wall looking for my next tool of torture.

I already know what I want to grab, but I stayed in a trance just scanning the wall in front of me, just in case I do decide to change my mind. I gave it a few moments, and my excited mind was clear on what I've been excited about. I reached up and pulled down a bone saw from the wall. The bone saw was extremely sharp. The jagged teeth on the blade were hungry to cut into something. The saw was all stainless steel, shiny and clean, except for the handle. The curved handle was made of wood. Wood that was starting to age. Most likely from the number of times it's been cleaned.

I felt its power run through my body as I held onto the handle tightly. This might kill him, but honestly, I don't care at this point. This is strictly for me. I also picked up the torch lying on the table, just in case this will prolong the torture. If I cauterize the cuts when I'm done, there's a chance I could finish what I want to do. Again, I don't give a shit.

I took the saw and torch and headed back over to John. He was looking around, almost blindly. He's acting like he has no idea where he is or what's happening anymore. I reached into the drawer to pull out a packet of smelling salts.

"I need you to snap out of it and wake up John." I said, as I popped the salts and waved them under his nose. "I'm still not done with you."

John came to and took a long deep breath as he shook his head weakly. He was still extremely weak and exhausted, but the fear in his eyes came back fully alive. I discarded the salts and held the saw in front of his face.

"That's better John." I said, looking into his eyes. "I want you to watch and pay attention, or I'll make you watch."

I moved the saw from his face and went around his body to each limb.

"Eeny, meany, miny, mo." I sang out loud.

I finally stopped the saw right below the knee, at the tibia area of the leg. I aligned the saw roughly 10 cm from the joint line and got myself ready to cut. As I made the motion to move my hand back to make the first incision, I saw John wince and close his eyes, looking away.

"Hey!" I called out. "I've told you to watch and pay attention or I'll make you. You really want to test me? I already took your tongue for not shutting your fucking mouth. I'm not kidding around!"

Without making a sound, John turned his head to face me, and he looked down at his knee.

"You need to trust me." I began, laughing. "I'm a doctor after all."

I continued to laugh as I once again got myself into position to start cutting below the knee. I moved my hand back and forth, listening as the saw cut through the bone. The sound of flesh getting ripped apart and the grinding of the bone were music to my ears. Blood spurted out from the incision and traveled down the table to the drip pan below.

John made gruesome noises. Loud intakes of breaths, groans, hisses, and hiccup sobs as I moved faster with my sawing. His eyes were finally huge, taking in the fact that he was losing his leg. Tears and sweat were pouring down his face. His face was turning whiter than a ghost.

I finally finished sawing off his left leg and quickly grabbed the torch. I used the torch to heat up the rounded tool that I used on Molly.

"Well, isn't this sweet." I spoke. "This is the tool I used on sweet Molly."

I continued to heat the tool while looking at John's face to see his reaction to my last comment. He was crying uncontrollably. The tool was finally ready, and I placed it right on the exposed joint.

The tool started to singe the flesh surrounding the joint. The blood flow slowly came to an end, and the air smelled of burning flesh once again.

"Mhmm." I said, looking at John's face. "Smells like success."

I decided to give John a little bit of time, as I contemplated my result. I'm going to work on his right leg next, but I don't know if I want to waste my time stopping the blood this time or let him slowly bleed out and just watch. I stood there thinking and staring at John. He looks awful, even worse than before. I really did a number on him this evening.

I was starting to get bored once again. The excitement was slowly leaving me. I hate when this happens. My impulse will take over, and then I'll have to move on to my next victim.

I raised the saw to John's right leg, right below the knee, and started sawing back and forth once again. What I thought would happen happened. My impulse took over, and I started sawing faster, out of control. I sawed so fast I ended up sawing nothing. I was done before I knew it, watching the blood flow out of the wound.

I set the saw down, feeling a little bit exhausted. I took a step back and decided to just let John bleed out. I continued to watch the blood leave his body. He wasn't making much noise or movement at this point. His body and mind must be spent by now. His face was getting even whiter by the second, and his lips were turning a pale color along with being extremely chapped.

I admired my work as I stood there just waiting for him to die. I was getting impatient and decided to take my pictures now. I went to the back and grabbed my camera. When I picked up the camera, I walked back over to John. While standing in front of him, I took several shots at various angles. As each photo came out of the camera, I placed them on the table next to him.

John was still breathing ever so slightly. It seemed like he was refusing to die. I was getting tired of watching the inevitable. I was completely bored at this point. I'm ready for my next victim. A new chapter in my story.

I decided to grab the knife I got from Frank's shop. It was time to finally end John's life. Not that I cared honestly, but this was taking too long, and I don't leave my victims breathing before I leave.

I grabbed the knife, took it out of its sheath, and stood above John on the side of the table.

"Okay, John boy." I said, looking down at him. "Goodbye."

I raised the knife high above his heart and struck hard and fast. More blood left where I inserted the knife as I quickly twisted and pulled the knife out from his chest.

I set the bloodied knife down on the table and glanced at John one last time. He finally took his final breath as his eyes stared off endlessly. He was finally dead, and my fun came to an end. At least for now.

Chapter Twenty-One: Julie

I was getting tired of wandering around, searching for Molly. It was getting later in the day, closer to evening. I've been at this for hours. What happened to Molly? Where did she go?

So many questions ran through my mind. Where are John and Mike? I feel like Mike would stop by Frank's store to see if he's seen Molly. If he's not there, he might have met up with John by the lake. Hopefully. I'll swing by Frank's shop first, then head to the lake.

My legs were killing me as I turned in the direction towards the shop. At least the temperature today was nice. It's been about 75 degrees the whole day, with a slight breeze. The sun was the only thing that was making today comfortable, but once the sun goes away, the breeze will make it feel chilly.

I continued to make my way towards the shop, watching the leaves in the trees sway back and forth slightly. The sound of the birds chirping away in the background gave off a peaceful vibe. It was gorgeous out. It would be beautiful if Molly weren't missing.

The shop finally came into view, and I started to walk faster. After a couple of minutes, I was almost to the door. As I approached, I reached for the door handle out of instinct, instead of reading the sign first, but the door didn't budge. I'm glad no one was around watching me. I felt silly for a moment. I then stepped back and read the sign: **CLOSED**.

That's odd that it's closed. It's not super late in the day. I peeked in the windows and peered inside. The store was completely empty. It didn't look like anyone has been in there for a while. Maybe the store was dead all day, and Frank decided to go home for the day. A feeling of defeat washed over me but decided to shake it off. I'll head towards the lake; I'm sure the boys will be there.

I turned away and headed towards the lake. A wave of new optimism rushed over me. I was really hoping they were there and had found Molly, or at least had the satisfaction of running into someone. I doubt they went back to the cabin without finding me first, but if they're not at the lake, I'll check the cabin after.

I followed the path towards the lake. The path was completely covered by trees. Such a beautiful trail, only to be clouded by a miserable situation. The breeze started to pick up a little as the day was getting later. I should have had a hoodie or a jacket with me just in case I would get chilly, but instead I pulled my flannel shirt sleeves down, covering up the goosebumps that were forming.

I finally arrived at the lake and took a minute to look around in search of the boys. I didn't see anyone in the surrounding area but heard voices coming from inside the shed. I walked towards the shed and heard muffled voices. It seemed like they belonged to John and Mike, but I wasn't sure.

I went to reach for the door handle and slightly twisted the knob, only to come to find it locked. I was about to knock on the door, but I wasn't completely sure if it was the boys or not. I couldn't be too careless, especially with Molly missing. I'm not about to take a chance. I decided to try and find an opening through a window so I could possibly see inside and be certain if it was the boys or not.

I walked to every window surrounding the shed and finally found a peephole on one of the windows. I carefully got close to the window and looked through the hole.

As I peeked through the hole, I saw two men in the room. One was standing with his back to me, blocking the face of the other man. I could tell that the other man was lying on the table. What the hell is going on? From this point of view, I couldn't tell what was happening or who the two men were.

The man moved just a little bit, and I saw whoever was lying on the steel table. I then was able to see that the man was strapped to the table. I still couldn't see any of their faces. A sense of fear rushed over me as I tried to maintain my composure. That must be the man that took Molly, but who does he have on the table now? I hope it's not John or Mike. Please no. I really should go seek help, but I'm intrigued to see if it is my boyfriend or my friend on that table.

I continued to look through the hole and wait till I could see their faces. The man standing up was waving his hands around, laughing. The man eventually headed towards the back of the shed, leaving the man on the table to come into view.

"Oh my God." I muttered to myself quietly. "John."

John was the one laying on the table, strapped down. He has blood coming out of his mouth and looks like his tongue is missing. The other man approached a filing cabinet in the corner of the back wall. I watched him go through the files inside and pulled something out. They looked like photos. Oh my. Did this guy take pictures of people as he tortured them?

My mind started going crazy. Was Molly in here? Where's Mike? Was this happening the entire time, right in front of us?

The man finally turned around, bringing the photos with him. As he got closer, my heart nearly dropped out of my chest. I couldn't believe my eyes. I was in complete shock.

"Mike!" I whisper-yelled to myself. What the fuck is he doing? I thought my mind was racing a minute ago; it's surely doing a number now. Has it been Mike the entire time?

I felt like I was going to be sick. Was that the whole reason he brought us out here? Why? He's always been so sweet. A good guy. I stayed watching Mike, still confused and shocked. He took the photos and waved them in front of John's face as he set them down on the table next to him. I watched him laugh as he went through each photo; he's acting like such a madman. What has happened to him? That's his best friend!

Mike went over to the table on the side of the shed and was rummaging through stuff. I saw him pull something out and reach over to grab what looked like a battery and cables. I should try and help John, but I just don't know how. I should run for help, but I'm in shock. I don't know what to do but stand right here and watch. I'm not able to move. I can't feel anything; that's how stunned I am. I want to cry, but I can't even do that.

As Mike made his way back to John, he set the battery and cables down on the table next to him. He held up the other item, and I could make out what it was. It was a pair of pliers. What was he going to do with those? Before I could start pondering its purpose, Mike took John's face with one hand and took the pliers straight to his face. He inserted the pliers, as he started twisting and pulling. By the time he managed to take the first tooth out, I turned my head and closed my eyes in disgust.

I fought the urge to vomit as I kept my eyes closed for another moment. When I looked back through the hole, Mike was laughing as he moved in for another tooth. Only this time he moved quicker as his rage took over. He must have taken out at least five teeth from John's mouth. When I saw the blood pour out of John's mouth and Mike dance around as he was enjoying himself, I turned my head once more. This time I lost it and threw up a bit. I tried to be as quiet as possible. I didn't want to get caught out here.

When I pulled myself together, I looked through the hole once more. Mike continued to dance and wave his hands around. It almost looks like he's playing around with the teeth resting on the table. John looks awful. You can see him sobbing with tears streaming down his face.

Mike composed himself and reached for the cables attached to the battery. I watched as he assembled the cables on John, and then suddenly, John started shaking and twitching uncontrollably.

After a few moments, Mike unhooked the cables from John and stood back, staring down at him. He had this evil smirk on his face, followed by a contemplating glance. I watched him walk to the back after putting away the battery and cables. When he reached the back, he looked so weak and so pale. I still ask myself why I didn't try to do something? Why haven't I run to seek help? I'm glued to what's happening. Is it the shock that's making me feel so helpless?

As if I were hypnotized, I studied Mike's behavior. He stared at that wall for a very long time. He stood straight as possible with one arm folded with the other in a thinking position with his hand to his mouth. I don't know what he's thinking about, but I most definitely don't like what I'm seeing.

After what seemed like an eternity, I saw Mike reach up to grab something off the wall. His back covered what he grabbed, so I didn't get to see what it was. As he took it down from the wall, I saw him study it for a few moments. As he turned around, his evil grin grew large, and then I saw what he held in his hands. The object in his hands looked like a very sharp saw.

I grimaced at the idea of him hacking John to bits. I still don't know why I can't break free from this shocked state of mind. I remained right where I was, as Mike walked back to John. As he approached him, he reached into a drawer and pulled something out and placed it under John's nose. John suddenly came to as I saw him snap to full attention. I've seen this before, at some of their baseball games with some of the athletes. I assumed it was smelling salts.

Once John was alert and was looking around, I saw Mike look down at him, waving his arms around. It looked like Mike was yelling something at John. John turned and looked at Mike as Mike steadied the saw once more.

Oh my. Mike was about to cut John's leg off! This is ridiculous! I was able to close my eyes, as Mike started cutting. I could hear the muffled cries coming from John. I was deeply disturbed at this point.

When I opened my eyes again, I saw Mike standing back. The smile on his face showed me how much enjoyment he gets out of this. On the other hand, John looked defeated, like he had nothing left in the tank.

I watched as Mike's expression changed quite rapidly. He went from excited to stone-like, like he was annoyed or agitated. He picked up the saw and started on the other leg.

You can tell by his facial expression; this was a whole other emotion coursing through his body. He moved faster with hate and impulse.

In a matter of seconds, he cut through John's other leg. I watched as Mike took a step back. Again, his emotions went from enjoyment to anger very quickly. I saw Mike make his way back to the table at the back of the shed. When he turned around, he had a camera in his hands.

"Son of a bitch!" I thought to myself as Mike walked back over to John lying helplessly and defeated.

I can't believe he's taking pictures of people on the table. It's obvious this isn't the first time, if he waved photos in front of John in the beginning. Were there photos of Molly?

Mike stood in front of John, snapping picture after picture. He would set each photo down on the table as it came out of the camera. After a few moments, Mike put the camera down again and took a step back to stare at John.

It seemed like Mike was still upset, since he threw his hands in the air, like he was a child, and stomped over to the side table once more. He turned around with a knife in his hands, and in a matter of seconds, he stabbed John in the chest.

I popped my head back and gave out a quiet shriek. When I placed my head back in the hole, it almost looked like John was staring at me through glazed-over eyes. He didn't blink anymore, and his chest stopped moving. When I assumed he was dead, I tweaked a little and stumbled on the cement block I was standing on. It must have made a loud enough sound, because when I looked again through the hole, I saw Mike turning around, looking in my direction. I didn't hesitate. I turned, got off the cement block completely, and ran in the direction towards the cabin. My flight mode finally kicked in, and I was not going to become the next victim.

Chapter Twenty-Two: "Mike"

It was about time for me to leave the shed. I'm already craving my next victim. I wonder if Mike's pretty little girl toy is at the cabin yet. As I started contemplating the things I would do to her, I heard a noise coming from outside. I quietly snuck to the window and looked through the hole in the window.

"Shit." I said, watching Julie run towards the path.

I started wondering how much she saw. She probably saw me through this exact hole in the window. I didn't hesitate; I reached for my hatchet and swung open the door.

Julie had a head start on me, but I figured she was headed towards the cabin. All our stuff is there. She couldn't make it far without her stuff. I bet she's going to search for the car keys, which are right here in my pocket.

This put a halt on planning what I was going to do to her, but this could be fun also. I picked up my pace a bit, hatchet in hand.

"Here kitty, kitty, kitty." I called out to Julie. "Where you going babe?"

She was a pretty fast runner. I lost sight of her quickly. Alright, so you want to have some fun. I like playing hide 'N' seek. It was getting closer to nighttime as the sun was starting to set and the moon started to become apparent. It was getting chillier out. No longer that beautiful 75 degrees. If I had to guess, it was probably more like 70 or 68 degrees out.

I started to slow down. I can hear the rustle sounds of the trees and the animal noises in the distance. The sounds I was searching for, what I was training my ears to pick up, were the sounds of twigs snapping or gravel getting churned up. There was a faint sound ahead that sounded like someone running, but I wasn't completely sure. The sound came in the direction heading back towards the cabin. At least she didn't go off the path to give me a challenge. To the cabin it is.

I continued down the path, getting closer to the cabin. I was keeping my ears trained to the specific noises just in case she did tear off from the path. Only a few moments later, I neared the end of the path, looking up at the nearby cabin. I don't see Julie anywhere outside the cabin. Maybe she already made it inside.

I finally approached the front door to the cabin and opened it slowly, listening carefully to any movement. The cabin was dead silent. Some kind of sound would be nice. This is starting to get irritating. There's nowhere that she can go. I'll eventually catch up to her. I'll make her pay for interrupting my fun. I'm going to take my time with her.

"Julie." I called out. "Come out, come out, wherever you are."

I stepped through the door and closed it behind me. I turned the lock on it as it closed. Usually, a victim tries to open the door first if they are running; fear and shock take place, making them freeze up and forget to check the lock. By the time the shock starts to disappear, the person chasing will close in. By that time, they would choose to run in a new direction. I've seen this happen countless times.

I walked towards the living room area and listened carefully, as I scanned the room. There was no sign of her. I walked into the dining room and then into the den. Yet again, I came up short. Where the hell is this bitch? I continued to survey the downstairs of the cabin, and I still came up empty.

"You have nowhere to go." I called out once more. "Come on out and play Julie."

I finished searching downstairs and decided to check upstairs. I headed over to the stairs and moved silently up each step. I clenched the hatchet in my hand, ready to strike if necessary.

As I climbed each step, I looked up to see if I could see her. The anxiety and anticipation raced through me like a strong current through a wire. I can't wait to get my hands on her. I want to feel her neck in between my hands as I squeeze hard, listening to her labored breathing, then letting go for her to regain her breath. The thought brought a smirk across my face.

I made it to the top of the stairs and strained my eyes through the darkness of the cabin. The cabin is now dark since the sun has finally set, and the moonlight doesn't hit this side of the cabin yet. No lights are on inside either. At least Julie was smart about that. She'll hide in the shadows, instead of creating shadows. This will make it harder for me to spot her, but there are not many hiding places she can be in.

I walked down the hallway, making my way towards John and Molly's room. Before I entered the room, I checked under the bed and in the closet, but Julie wasn't in this room. I did a once-over again to double-check the dark places.

When I came up empty once more, I left the room. I made my way over to the bathroom to check in there. I didn't bother turning on the light. I prefer hunting in the dark. I pulled open the shower curtain quickly, raising my hatchet to strike.

Of course, the shower was empty. Julie wasn't hiding here. She's smarter than she looks. This pissed me off and I slammed my fist on the shower wall in disappointment.

"Julie!" I exclaimed. "Let's play a game. Come on!"

I spun around to leave the bathroom. The only place left is Mike and Julie's room. She must be hiding in there. There's nowhere else to check. There is a possibility that she's not even in here, and I wasted all this time, giving her plenty of time to get ahead of me. I shook my head at the thought. No. She would have come to the cabin first to figure out her next move.

I left the bathroom and made my way to the last room. Entering the bedroom, I looked around to find an empty room. She must be in this bathroom. It's the last place to check in this cabin.

"Julie!" I exclaimed. "You're starting to piss me off!"

I entered the bathroom and walked straight to the shower. I flung open the curtain with my hatchet raised once again. Julie wasn't in here either. The shower was empty.

"Fuck!" I cried out.

I started to turn around when I felt something hard hit my head, then I heard a voice.

"You're starting to piss me off too." Julie yells as she hits the back of my head.

The pain raced through my body. My head instantly hurt. Whatever she used to strike me hurt like hell. My eyesight became weak and hazy quickly as I fell to the floor. Before I knew it, I was out cold.

Chapter Twenty-Three: Julie

I ran as fast as I could after jumping off the cement block. I glanced behind me and saw the door fly open. I heard Mike call after me, as I continued to run. I started running down the path, heading back to the cabin.

It was getting darker out as the sun was beginning to set. It wasn't as warm out anymore without the much-needed heat from the sun. The breeze picked up a bit more, bringing me chills. Once again, I wished I had a jacket; it's going to get colder once the sun is completely gone.

Not only am I feeling colder, but it is also hard to see anything. I can't really see behind me to tell how far behind Mike is. I didn't have a flashlight or my cell phone with me. One of the reasons why I need to go to the cabin. I need my phone. Not only do I need my phone, but maybe I could also find the car keys in the cabin as well. Now, I need to find help. It's going to be harder to get help since I got myself busted.

I should have run away a lot sooner, but I couldn't shake the state of shock. I'm still in shock, but now I'm able to run away. I continued to run almost blindly down the path towards the cabin, hoping to get as much separation from

Mike as possible. As I ran, I shook my head, trying to shake off the disbelief that Mike could do all of this.

I could still hear Mike running after me as I continued to get closer to the cabin. I feel as if I'm getting closer, but it seems like a lifetime ago that I left the shed. My surroundings sounded eerie. There were animal noises coming from both sides of me. Along with the animal noises, the leaves dance with the wind, as it slightly blows, creating that creepy, swishing noise. My fear is at an all-time high currently, and my anxiety is causing me to sweat regardless of the chills I have from the change in temperature.

After a few moments, I finally caught a glimpse of the cabin. I ran as fast as I could towards the front door. As I approached the front door, I swung it open and shut it quickly. I thought about running around to find the keys and my phone, but I've seen too many horror movies to know I'll never have enough time to be successful. Mike would come through that door before you know it. Instead, my first instinct is to find a weapon; if I can take him out first, then I can focus on the other necessities. It's a long shot, but if I have surprise on my side, maybe I can pull this off. He would be too worried that I would be a dumb female and make all the mistakes.

Mike would probably feel like I'd be hiding in an obvious area. Somewhere he could easily find me and then take me back to torture me. Instead, my action plan is to find something quick to strike him and try to follow behind him to come up and strike him fast.

I thought quickly and hard. What can I use that will be fast and quick? As I raced through my thoughts, I landed on the fire poker resting in its place by the hearth. I hurried over to the living area near the fireplace. My heart was racing a mile a minute. I reached down and grabbed the black steel. It felt cool between my hands. As I grabbed the poker, I studied its length as I held it straight up. I also studied its weight as I gave it a couple practice swings. When I became content with the weapon of choice, I then decided it was time to find a hiding place. Time was of the essence. It's only a matter of time until Mike opens that door. Now that I have my weapon, I need to focus on my breathing, stealth, and the ability to maintain a safe distance behind Mike.

Mike still hasn't entered the front door yet, which I found odd. It felt like a lifetime ago since I entered through that door, but my anxiety probably slowed time down. Without thinking, I flew up the stairs. I ran through possible scenarios in my head.

He would probably check downstairs first, then head up the stairs to check the floor up here. I would have to move from room to room stealthily for this to work. The first room he would check is John and Molly's. Maybe if I hid in the farthest bathroom, I could circle back to their room after he's checked it.

I entered the bathroom and hid behind the door; just in case, he would most likely check the shower first if he did come straight to the bathroom. This bathroom was a decent-sized room since it's considered the main bathroom, so hiding behind the door would be easy. All I would have to do is control my breathing and try to remain quiet.

As I stood there, controlling my breathing, I finally heard the front door open, followed by the lock on the door latching. He thinks I haven't trained my ears to pay attention to small details like that. Mike clearly hasn't paid much attention to my IQ. All I can do right now is maintain my breathing and train my ears to every movement. I must get this right. I need to survive.

As he entered, I heard him call out to me, taunting me. Cute, but come and find me, asshole. I thought he liked games after all. I heard him walk into the living room area of the cabin. After a few brief moments, he continues to each room. First the dining area, and then the den.

I then heard him call out once more, still thinking he has the upper hand taunting me. I then heard him head towards the stairs. He thinks he's being careful coming up each step, but I know exactly where he is. The one thing he's taught me is to know my surroundings very well. Hell, he probably been sneaking out every night the same way he's sneaking up the stairs. The only difference now is that I'm wide awake, paying attention.

I can tell the sun is now pretty much set, the hall is dark, and I can't see much. I can use that to my advantage as well. It doesn't seem like he has a light and is traveling by moonlight himself. This will make it easy for me to lurk in the shadows behind him, unless he does turn on a light. I have a strong impression that he won't, since he's probably thinking the same thing. Moving and hiding in the shadows is the game we will play.

I heard him reach the top of the stairs. He probably didn't even realize that the top made a small squeak as he planted the second foot down at the top. He would be too worried thinking he has the upper hand. Again, I'm just a dumb female, remember?

By now, I'm sure he's made his way towards the first bedroom, which would be John and Molly's; off to the side, I heard the closet door open. I knew for a fact he was in their bedroom.

What shocked me was the fact that I heard footsteps approach this bathroom. I sucked in a breath and steadied myself. Even though my heart was trying to beat out of my chest. I did everything in my power not to completely freak out. I held my emotions in check as Mike stepped into the room.

I remained behind the door, holding the fire poker as tight as can be, as he barged in. As expected though, he didn't turn on the light, which probably saved me.

I heard the shower curtain get pulled to the side quickly. I stayed as still as possible; now is not the time to strike. I'll wait till he's in our room to do that if I make it that far.

Suddenly, I heard a loud bang on the shower wall. He slammed his fist on the wall. An act of defeat. I then heard him call out my name in aggravation, followed by another taunt. I could tell that he refused the feeling of defeat.

After a moment, I heard him leave the room. I mean come on. For a murderer, he wasn't the brightest. I expected so much more out of Mike. You must check behind the door, but I guess that's what he gets when you mix anticipation, excitement and adrenaline together, along with not bothering to turn the light on.

I listened as he left the room. The only spot he would go next would be our room. He checked the closet in John and Molly's room, so I expected him to do the same in ours. After the obvious spots would come the bathroom. After I hear the closet door open and shut, that will be my time to attack.

After a short moment, I heard Mike exclaim in rage, annoyance and anger. He called my name with authority. I could tell he was starting to get pissed off, as he was running out of rooms to check. I could only imagine the feeling of thinking he was going to finally find me hiding in our bathroom. Oh, what a dumb asshole he is.

I then heard an angry "Fuck!" come out of him. He flung open the shower curtain only to find it empty. I successfully managed to get behind him and watch his failed attempt at finding me. I'm not going to lie; it brought a smile to my face. I outsmarted him at his own game.

As he started to turn around, I swung hard and fast with the fire poker; I struck him right on the back of his head. It felt good. A sigh of relief rushed over me. I felt myself relax a little bit and call out, "You're starting to piss me off too!"

As I struck fast and hard, I watched as he slowly fell to the floor. I was relieved my plan worked. I was almost proud of myself. I watched Mike fall to the floor, knocked out from the blow. I thought for a split second about searching him for the car keys and to run to find my phone, but in a split second I had a rush of a different idea. I almost chuckled at myself at the thought of the irony at my feet.

Chapter Twenty-Four: Julie

I wanted to go find help, but I thought to myself that there are other things I wanted to do. Mike is lying in front of me unconscious. Maybe I can find my own justice for the time being. With this revelation, I smiled at myself. I don't know where I'm going to end up, but I figured someone should show him a taste of his own medicine.

I thought to myself where I could stick him for the time being. It's only me, that is. No one will come to help. It's a small town. Actual help would take too long to get here. I should keep him up here, since I would struggle too much to get him down the stairs by myself.

I then thought to myself, what would I tie him to and to what? We do have a headboard I can contain him with. I smirked at the irony of the idea, as Mike always wanted to incorporate being tied to a headboard as some kind of foreplay. I was never interested in that until now.

All I must do now is find a way to tie him to the bed. I thought long and hard about that question. Once again, time was of the essence. I want to make sure he's secured before I'm able to take my time. For now, I must be quick on my feet before he becomes conscious and wakes up. He'll be able to overpower me, injury and all. I would be no match against him.

I racked my brain till a fast, easy solution came to mind. I'm sure there's some duct tape somewhere downstairs. I turned to run down the steps towards the kitchen.

As I entered the kitchen, I started to open drawers as fast as I could to find the tape. I made my way around the kitchen, opening as many cabinets as possible. I didn't bother to close any of them shut when I was done. I was on my last drawer and finally found a roll of tape. It was in a drawer with a bunch of random items of use.

When I grabbed the roll, I turned to leave the kitchen, leaving the kitchen a mess. I rounded the corner towards the stairs and took multiple steps at a time back to our room. I set the roll on the nightstand next to the bed. I walked into the bathroom and grabbed Mike's ankle.

To my astonishment, he was still unconscious. Awesome, I thought to myself. I reached down and grabbed both of his legs and tried to turn him around towards the bedroom. Man, that was a lot of work. He weighed almost twice the amount I weighed. With determination and adrenaline, I put all my might into it. I managed to turn him around and dragged his sorry ass towards the bed.

As I approached the bed, I let go of his feet to catch a breather. Man, I was tired! I have no idea how I'll get him up on the bed. I'm just hoping with all the adrenaline I have, I'll be able to toss him onto the bed. All the while, he remains unconscious. I took a moment to catch my breath. As I thought of all the stuff he possibly did, thanks to witnessing firsthand all the horrible things he's done to John, I managed to get his body up on the bed. Don't ask me how, but I managed to do it all by myself. All his dead weight took a toll on me. I was out of breath, and that takes a lot, since I'm very athletic and in top shape.

As I positioned his body, I grabbed one arm and held it against the bed frame. With my other hand, I undid some tape and used my mouth to unfasten it from the roll. I took the tape and secured his first wrist to the bedframe. Now that I had one fastened, the second wrist should be easier. I undid some tape the same way and applied it to the second wrist. After I secured both wrists, I went around multiple times, just to make sure they were completely secure. I can't take any chances; I made it this far. I don't want him to easily escape.

After both wrists were completely secure to the bedposts, I moved on to his feet. I grabbed one ankle with one hand and took some tape off the roll with the other. Once again, I used my teeth to tear off the first set. I secured his first ankle to the bedpost and moved on to the next.

After I made sure each part of his wrists and ankles was triple wrapped to the bedposts. I was fully satisfied. I knew there wasn't a way for him to break free unless he was on some kind of drug that would let him bust loose easily.

I sat back and admired my work and skills. I still couldn't believe this all worked. I was able to knock him out and tie him to the bed. I now have the chance to call for help and turn him in, but I have my own plans for him.

I remembered Mike showing pictures to John as he was torturing him. I want to be able to go and look for myself. What exactly was he capable of? I still can't believe he's still knocked out. I must have hit him hard.

I was pretty content with him lying here. I feel like I did a solid job at tying him down to the bed. It was a risk I was willing to take. First though, I'm going to check his pockets for the keys. I'll need the keys for the car at some point.

I searched his pockets till I found the set of keys. I slipped them into my own pocket and got myself ready to head down to the shed.

I flew down the stairs toward the front door. As I expected, Mike did lock the door. That might have worked on anyone else, but I'm prepared for this, thanks to Mike. He made me watch every horror movie possible whenever we had the time to, in between classes and sports. Especially in October.

I unlocked the door but stopped. I just remembered how dark it was. I'll need a flashlight to see. I left the door open and headed towards the kitchen once more.

I remembered seeing a flashlight in one of the drawers I left open. I entered the kitchen and headed straight to the drawer. I reached down and grabbed the flashlight. I then checked it out. I turned it on and off a few times, and I was good to go. I then headed back to the open door to the front of the cabin.

I exited the door, turned on the flashlight and headed down the path towards the shed. I didn't think twice; I was determined to see exactly what kind of animal I was working with.

I was sure that Mike wasn't going to go anywhere. I put a ton of duct tape on him. There was no way he could break through the tape. As I hurriedly went down the path, my mind wasn't concerned about Mike. It was concerned about what I was about to find. John would still be lying on the table when

I get there, and I would have to prepare myself to find him dead. It would be a lot different seeing him dead up close than from a tiny hole in the window.

The sun was completely gone now, and the moon was out high above. It was pitch black, and all I had was the light from this flashlight. I slightly jump at every movement that I hear. Even though Mike is back at the cabin, I'm terrified something will jump out at me.

My anxiety was causing me to sweat once again, and my increased heart rate warmed me up. If it weren't for that, I would feel the coolness from the breeze that was starting to pick up. I continued to walk faster as I began my approach to the shed. I can see the table and the building come into view.

I let out a small sigh of relief that I was finally there but am still not excited that I'm in this situation. I reached the door to the shed and paused for a moment. Nothing I can do will prepare me to face the reality lying in front of me.

I took a long, deep breath as I held the handle. A chill ran down my spine, letting me feel the coolness from the atmosphere. I shivered and closed my eyes for a second. I twisted the handle, opened my eyes and opened the door.

As I entered, I shut the door behind me and locked it just in case. I stared at John lying on the table, brutally tortured.

Blood was pooled under the table. I wiped a tear away from my eyes as I walked over to him.

"I'm so sorry John." I whispered to him, feeling guilty I didn't do anything to help him.

I cleared my mind quickly. I was there for a reason and wanted to hurry up and get out of there as fast as possible. I took one last glance at John with teary eyes and turned away. I moved the flashlight over to the corner of the shed near the back in search of the filing cabinet. As the filing cabinet lit up in the beam of the light, I made my way over to it. I carefully walked over to it. When I stood in front of the cabinet, I took a deep breath and prepared myself for what I was about to find.

I hesitated for another moment and reached for the first drawer with shaky hands. I managed to slide open the top drawer as my hand continued to tremble. I looked inside and noticed there were tabs separating the files. I was frozen with horror as I read the tabs. There's a ton of information inside the cabinet on those that fell victim to Mike. What I couldn't grasp was the number of names inside. How the hell did he have time for all these people? I pulled out the **Photos** tab and opened the file. There were dozens of photos inside the file. I grabbed the most recent ones, and as I expected, they were pictures of John. Images of him brutally tortured.

Behind the photos of John were pictures of Frank. Oh my God! No wonder why the store was closed. The poor old man looked horrible in the photos. I couldn't stand looking at them.

I was about to put the photos away when something caught my eye. The photos behind Frank's were of Molly. No! Not Molly too. I fell into shock and started to cry deeply. Tears were running down my face. These are probably the photos that the sick fuck was shoving in John's face. I only brought myself to look at one of the images. That was enough for me. I felt the urge to throw up as I started to gag as I continued to cry hysterically. I was trying to control my breathing in between each hiccup and gag. I couldn't control my heart rate or the feeling of being sick. This was all too much to take in.

The images of all three will forever be implanted in my mind. I threw the file back into the cabinet and reached for the **ID** tab. My hands were shaking out of control and my vision remained blurry from the tears swelling up. I set the folder down on top of the cabinet since I could barely hold on to it. As I opened the file, there were dozens of pages of photocopied IDs. They were all women. Every single paper in here was a female and I can bet that the rest of the photos would match these IDs.

I'm absolutely horrified by my findings. Suddenly my emotions grew straight into anger. My breathing finally slowed down and I stopped crying. I have so much hate for the person I thought I loved. All these poor girls need retribution and I'm planning on giving just that to every single one of them. I will be their voice and weapon. I will seek their revenge for them. I no longer thought about seeking help. I don't need it. I already got Mike right where I want him, and I would have to wait forever for someone to come anyway. I will be judge, jury, and executioner myself.

I sat there for a moment and thought about if I had what it took to seek justice myself for all the victims and my rage burning inside me gave me the reassurance I needed. I can and I will. The next question that came to mind was how to do it. I should use one of his tools against him. Give him some more ironic medicine to shove down his throat. I'm not sure if my stomach can handle what I'm about to do, but I'm sure my will is strong enough to complete the task at hand. I walked over to the back wall and shone the flashlight across the wall. I was scanning the wall trying to figure out the perfect weapon for the much-needed sweet justice.

I continued to scan the wall, examining each of the tools hanging in its place on the wall. I paused for a second once a pair of hedge clippers came into view. I gave a little smirk as

I thought that would be perfect. I know exactly what I want to use these for. Don't worry ladies, I will finally give you the peace you deserve.

I reached up and grabbed the clippers down from its hanging place. I held them tight in my hands for a moment, feeling the power flow through me. I have this sense of confidence rush through my body. Maybe it's the spirits of all the women that fell victim to Mike.

I turned around feeling a bit satisfied along with the strong feelings of sadness. I then walked over to John, still lying on the table. I looked down on him and stood briefly in silence.

"I'm so sorry." I said once again to John. "I'm going to make it right. For you. For Molly. And for all those that fell victim to that asshole. I promise you that."

Tears fell down my face once more as I continued to stare at John's dead, cold eyes. I wiped away the tears, sniffled back my emotions and cleared my throat. It was time to head back to the cabin and finally deal with the asshole. I shone the light on the floor as I made my way to the door of the shed. I didn't want to walk on something that I shouldn't. As I approached the door, I glanced one last time at John on the table, then closed the door. Ready to face my nightmare lying ahead of me.

Chapter Twenty-Five: "Mike"

I slowly came to. I blinked my eyes open slowly, feeling a sharp pain course through the back of my head, giving me an instant headache. I went to feel the area that caused me pain, but I was unable to move my hand. I'm still a bit delirious and haven't fully realized I was tied down. I attempted to move my other hand and yet again I couldn't move it. I then tried to move my legs and to no surprise, couldn't get them to move either. As I fully came to, I finally realized that both my hands and legs were secured to the bedposts. I warily looked around the room, blinking a couple more times. How the hell? I began to think to myself.

As I looked around the room, it was empty. I was all by myself. How did she get the upper hand over me? I'm never this reckless. I remember checking out the bathroom in the room and then bam! I got struck on the head. I wonder if she left to go get help. Will this be my downfall? As long as she's concerned, I'm still her almost-perfect boyfriend, Mike. She doesn't know the truth unless, instead of seeking help, she lets her imagination take over, searching for answers. If that was the case, then she would have to have gone back to the shed looking for the answers, and she would not like what she would come across.

The look on her face if she found out how many were killed and especially the truth as to what happened to her slut of a best friend came into clear focus. How I would kill more just to see that look of shock. That look of reality slapping right across her pretty face. I'm still pissed off that I'm in this situation. How the hell am I going to break out of this? I continued to try and wiggle my wrists and legs in hopes of breaking myself free. It was no good. She managed to put enough duct tape on me. I'm not going anywhere at this point.

I closed my eyes and listened to my background. It was still and quiet. It doesn't sound like she's here anymore. There wasn't a sound stirring. All the lights in the cabin were still off, leaving me in a pitch-dark room. I strained my eyes to see if I was able to see a glimpse of something, anything, but I was not able to make out anything. The only light shining through the room was that from the moon, high above in the sky. The moonlight cast a small shadow in the corner, making it seem like there is something just lurking in the corner.

The one time that I don't clean up after myself, I get myself into a situation like this. I've left both Frank and John right where they've spent their last moments. I didn't get a chance to finish and clean up. My impulses got the better of me, and all I wanted to do was go after my next victim.

As I laid there staring up at the ceiling, I finally heard a sound coming from downstairs. I listened carefully and it sounded like a door closing. Who has entered the house? Will it be Julie or the police coming to take me away? There was no urgency in the way the individual entered the house, so it must be Julie. There was no sound of heavy footsteps pounding their way up to the room; instead, it was quiet, soft footsteps.

After a few moments I managed to catch a figure entering the bedroom. It was a slender figure that entered the darkness. Well, it wasn't the police; it had to be Julie. As the figure moved farther into the room, I noticed the individual walking over to the nightstand near the bed. Suddenly, the room lit up as she turned on the light. It was indeed Julie. I was almost relieved it was her and not the police. There might be a chance of me getting out of this and finally getting my hands around her fucking throat.

Julie moved away from the lamp and hovered over me. She just stared down at me. I studied her face and was surprised to see the look in her eyes. She didn't look scared or hurt; she looked more pissed off than anything. Good girl. I knew she had it in her to show me that fiery side of her hiding deep down. I am interested in what turned her into this raging animal standing in front of me. As she got closer to me, I noticed she had something in her hand. They looked like gardening shears. What was she going to do with those? Does she have what it takes to torture me? She's been a precious little angel for as long as Mike knew her. I'm starting to get excited.

"Hello Mike." Julie said to me as she continued to look down at me.

I let out a small laugh as I noticed her grip the shears tighter as she spoke to me.

"Miss me?" I said, staring back at her.

Chapter Twenty-Six: Julie

For once I didn't feel a sense of urgency. I headed towards the path leading back to the cabin. I moved gingerly, feeling no reason to hurry back. I have my answers, a weapon for justice, and Mike is secured to the bedposts. There's no one around so I have plenty of time to make it back. I need to get my mind centered for me to successfully do what needs to be done. I can't let these girls down. Or John for that matter.

I continued to take my time walking down the path. All I have is the light from the flashlight illuminating the way. With each step, I strengthen my mind, thinking that I have what it takes to do what needs to be done. The air was more on the cooler side, with the slight breeze from earlier picking up the pace. Chills went down my spine and I gave off a constant shiver. I'm feeling the cold now that I'm less anxious.

The walk down the path seemed long, as the chills continued to flow through my body. Off in the distance I can hear all the nocturnal animals making their noises. The noises in the background seem to be clear as I'm zoned in. I'm still being cautious of other sounds just in case there's someone else out here lurking in the woods. I'm aiming the flashlight at the ground and slightly above the ground. I don't want to end up tripping on something along the path. I must keep myself as healthy and safe as possible if this is going to work.

After a few minutes of walking down the path in the cool dark environment, the cabin slowly came into sight. The anticipation started to rise, and my heart rate started to race. With every step I took, the more my heart would pound. I no longer feel the brisk air and my body started to heat. My rage started to take over and course strongly throughout my body.

As I carefully walked towards the front door of the cabin, I shown the light in the surrounding area. I want to make sure one last time I'm truly alone. After a moment of clarity, I walked up the small steps towards the front door. I took a deep breath and twisted the doorknob, opening the door.

I didn't bother worrying about closing the door quietly. I stood in the entrance and took a minute to listen to my surroundings. The cabin was completely silent. I moved away from the door and made my way over to the stairs, ready to make my climb to justice. I took my time walking up the stairs. I'm in no hurry. Hopefully he woke up and is contemplating how and why this happened to him, just like he's done to all his victims. I finally reached the top step and moved down the hall towards the bedroom. I entered the room and stood there for a moment. I can hear him twist and turn trying to figure out who entered the room. After a moment passed by, I walked over to the nightstand to turn on the light.

As the light illuminated the room, I turned and looked down at Mike. He was still fully secured to the bedposts. He was exactly how I left him. I stood over him and just stared. He had this stupid little smirk on his face, as if he's still in control. This fueled my rage, making me even more angry. I tighten the shears in my hand as I noticed him glance down to my hand.

"Hello Mike." I said glaring deep into his eyes.

I watched and listened as he started laughing at me.

"Miss me?" He asked smirking and glaring at me.

It seems like he's challenging me to do something rash. If he hasn't figured it out yet, I'm not going to make a mistake. I'm going to be collected and as calm as possible. I can't afford to make a mistake and let him regain the upper hand.

"I've been to the shed." I began. "I've seen everything that you've been up to."

"Oh yeah?" He said sarcastically. "And what exactly have I been up to?"

"Cut the shit. I've seen all the photos that you've taken." I continued. "All those poor girls."

"And how exactly do you know all of those were me?" He asked, looking up at me.

"You're seriously going to keep this up Mike?" I asked. "I've seen all the proof I need and saw it firsthand."

"Well now Julie." He started to say. "If you've seen me firsthand, why didn't you go for help?

"I was in shock!" I exclaimed. "I couldn't believe what I was seeing with my eyes! You of all people.

"Me of all people?" He mocked me. "And why is that so hard to believe?"

"I know you, Mike!" I yelled. "This isn't you! You're not capable of this."

"You're right about that babe." He spoke. "And that's where you're wrong."

"I'm not following." I protested. "How am I wrong? I told you I've seen all the proof I need."

"You're wrong, because Mike isn't capable of any of this." He began. "Well, I guess you're partly wrong and right."

"I'm not following." I stated, still confused.

"I'm not Mike." He said with a big smirk on his face. "He's been gone a long time."

"You're still not making any sense." I said, staring at him, lost. "What do you mean Mike is gone? You're right in front of me."

"Mike is right in front of you, but his mind has been gone for quite some time now." He explained. "I've taken over his mind shortly after he got here."

"Well, if you're not Mike, then who the hell do you claim to be then?" I asked in disbelief.

"I can tell that you think your dumb boyfriend has lost his mind." He said, chuckling. "I can assure you that it's not Mike that has been lying. I guess in a way he has lost his mind, but he's not to be blamed for any of this."

"That doesn't make any sense Mike!" I exclaimed. "You need some help. You're not making any sense."

"I'm not Mike!" He cried out. "My name is Dr. Jacob Underwood and I've taken control over your precious boyfriend."

"This coo of yours is not going to work on me Mike!"

"It's not a damn coo!" He said angrily. "Mike wouldn't be able to do any of this without me pulling all the strings. Did you happen to notice all the initials on the back of all the files in that cabinet?”

“No!” I cried out. “I saw enough and couldn’t bear anymore!”

“Then you’ve missed the initials J.U. on the back of all the files.”

I stood there for a moment staring and studying his face. His emotion and reaction look sincere. Either he’s completely gone mad, or he’s telling me the truth. A truth that doesn’t make any sense. I have no idea what he’s talking about. The one thing I know for sure is that there is no way Mike is capable of any of this. If what he’s telling me is true, there might be a chance to get Mike back. I just don’t know how.

“I know what you’re thinking.” He said, staring up at me.

“And what exactly is that?” I asked him.

“You’re wondering if I’m telling the truth or if Mike has gone completely mad.” He began to say. “I can assure you this is the truth, and I can also assure you there’s no way of getting Mike’s mind back.”

“I don’t believe you!” I said as a tear formed in my eye.

“I can’t make you believe me Julie.” He said, looking at me. “What I do know is as long as I have control of his mind, there's no chance of getting Mike back. This isn't the first mind I've taken over. I'm sure you've seen how far back those files have gone. There's no way Mike was able to do all of those."

"That was a troubling fact." I said in agreement, still not wanting to believe any of this.

"Mike was an easy mind to take control over." He continued to explain. "He also had the means to do what was necessary."

"What was necessary?" I asked him. "What were you trying to accomplish?

"That's easy." He said smiling. "Revenge."

"Revenge for what?" I asked.

"On this town for what they did to me all those years ago." He explained. "I'm not going to get into the entire story. I'm sure you can look it up. It's not a campfire story; it's reality. Here you are staring down reality right in its face."

"Why are you being so relaxed?" I asked. "I have you pinned down with nowhere to go. This is the end of the line for you!"

"You think this is the end of the road for me?" He said, laughing madly. "This will be the end of Mike, not for me."

"We'll see about that!" I said, watching him laugh uncontrollably.

"Oh yes, you will!" He responded sounding threatening. "So, what are you going to do?

"I'm going to get justice for all those poor women you've killed!" I exclaimed.

"All those poor women." He mocked me, continuing to laugh. "And how are you going to do that?

"I'm going to take these hedge clippers and take back something from your manhood!" I responded wildly.

"And you think that will stop me?" He asked.

I'm getting very curious as to why he keeps asking me why I think it'll stop him. I'm going to take away his manhood and watch him bleed out. He'll be dead very shortly and finally all his victims will have their justice and they could rest eternally. Yet, he's so calm and collected, as if none of this even matters to him. As if nothing fazes this guy.

"With these." I said, holding up the shears.

As I stood above him, his smirk was boiling my blood. My rage was building at an aggressive pace. I moved down towards his waist and pulled down his pants and his underwear in one swift motion. I couldn't believe my eyes.

This sick fuck was getting hard from this. He must really like torture. He's mad! There's no doubt in my mind that he doesn't deserve what' coming and I feel as if I can do this with ease. I raised the gardening shears towards his groin and took his penis in between the blades. I gave a swift motion with the shears and cut off his manhood quickly. As blood started to spurt out of the open wound, I immediately turned my head and threw up on the floor. The reality finally struck me and couldn't believe what I was able to do.

I continued to throw up and dry heave for a few more moments. My stomach was in knots. I don't know how certain individuals were able to do something like this. If it weren't for all those poor women, I would never be able to do something like this. As I composed myself, I wiped my mouth on my sleeve. I stood back up and didn't hear anything. Once I stood looking at him seeing the pool of blood form down by his groin area, I started to hear laughter. Are you serious?! This man is laughing at what happened? The laughter was short-lived though. After a few moments of nonstop laughter, everything went quiet. There was no way he already died from this.

A few seconds passed as the room remained silent, and then suddenly, I hear a huge gasp of air coming from Mike's body, followed by screams of agony. I studied the face of Mike and saw the amount of pain going through his body. I don't understand. One minute he laughed uncontrollably and now he's screaming in pain.

I continued to stare at Mike. Staring into his bugged-out eyes. He's looking around the room in full terror. This is completely different than before. Maybe the sicko does indeed feel pain after all. He certainly bleeds after all.

"Julie!" He cried out, letting out all his emotion of pain. "What the fuck are you doing?"

I stopped in complete shock. His tone was different, and it sounded like it was the old Mike. My Mike. Immediately tears formed in my eyes and my stomach turned sour. I felt the acid form in my esophagus.

"Mike?" I whispered weakly, the sound of garbled phlegm from the tears forming making it hard to understand what I said.

"What the fuck Julie." He repeated through gritted teeth, still feeling an enormous amount of pain. "Why am I tied up? And what the fuck! Why did you cut off my fucking dick?"

"I'm so sorry, baby!" I said as tears overwhelmed my face. "He said there would be no chance of you ever coming back?"

"What the fuck are you talking about?" He asked, still gritting his teeth from the pain. "Who said that?"

"The doctor!" I exclaimed. "The doctor told me that your mind was lost for good and that I would never get the chance to get you back!"

"What the fuck are you talking about?" He repeated.

"The doctor that took over your mind!" I began to explain. "He made you do terrible things! You don't remember anything?"

"You're not making any sense!" He cried out. "I don't remember anything!"

"It was a doctor that was killed here and before he died, he cursed the woods in order to take over someone's mind." I continued to explain. "And you were the chosen one this time."

"Why? Why me?" He asked confusedly. "What did he need me for?"

"He said you had the strength to do what was needed to be done." I continued. "He wanted to seek revenge and your mind was strong enough to get him to do what was necessary."

"So, you decided to cut my dick off?" He yelled.

"I thought you were the doctor!" I cried out, starting to bawl. "I wanted to get justice for all the women that he's tortured. He told me your mind was gone forever!"

"That's the stupidest thing I have ever heard!" He continued to yell. "I'm going to die!"

The blood continued to flow onto the bed, and I could tell he was getting weaker. His anger was primarily fueled by his adrenaline, trying to figure out the reality of the situation. Once his adrenaline wears off, he'll become even weaker. I'm afraid he doesn't have much time left. He's already lost so much blood. Instead of trying to stop the bleeding, we sat here explaining what was going on. Once again, the shock and emotions stopped me from helping out in the situation. I feel so stupid. I feel fooled. Now I'm going to lose the love of my life. I also feel so confused as to what transpired. So much has happened in such a short time.

Another thought popped in my head. Maybe it's the doctor fooling me again. Maybe he's saying these things to get me to help him. Make him survive. Maybe it is Mike, and he's thinking clearly again. He sounds so genuine. So sincere. I let out a dry heave once again and then threw up once more on the floor. I feel so sick to my stomach. I can't believe this is happening. It's a sick nightmare that's become a harsh reality.

"Mike." I managed to choke. "I'm so sorry. I love you so much!"

"I still don't understand what's happening." He started to say weakly. "Just know that no matter what, I'll always forgive you and that I will always love you."

I started to weep heavily. Uncontrollable tears streamed down my face. I was full of remorse and guilt. I wish that we had never come here. We should have gone down south with the rest of the college kids. Why did all this happen?

I peered over and threw up some more. I'm feeling extremely upset. I feel lost. I don't even know what I will do without Mike with me. I wiped my mouth with the sleeve of my shirt and tried to dry my tears. I looked down at Mike still lying on the table bleeding out. His face was turning white and his lips starting to turn blue. He doesn't have much longer, increasing my sense of depression.

Once again tears rushed to my eyes and streamed down on my face. I still can't believe my eyes.

"Julie." Mike said weakly.

"Yes, My love?" I said, choking out the words.

"I'm sorry for anything I've done. I would never do anything to hurt anyone." He managed to get out.

"I know Mike." I said, in-between hiccup sobs. "I know you would never do something like this. I forgive you Mike and I love you so much."

As I said this, I looked down at him and noticed his eyes stare up at the ceiling, no longer looking around. Just an empty stare. I checked for a pulse, but he's no longer here. I laid my head on his chest, feeling his empty body. It wasn't moving up or down. His heart was no longer beating. He was completely still. I've lost my love. I stayed there, right there on his chest, just letting out my sobs and screaming in remorse and agony. What did I do? He's gone forever now. The doctor was telling the truth. Mike would never come back to me. I just didn't think it would come down to this.

I glanced up, back at Mike's face. He's still looking up at the ceiling. A cold, eternal look that I would never forget. I placed my arms around him and just lay in silence for a bit longer.

Chapter Twenty-Seven: Dr. Jacob Underwood

I released Mike's mind for one reason only. I want him to feel the pain and suffering that he's about to experience. I'll still be able to enjoy the kind of torment and pain he's about to experience. Although it won't be my doing, I'm still going to enjoy as much of this as possible.

Even in the spiritual world, I have a huge smirk across my face. The stupid bitch didn't think it would be possible for Mike's mind to come back to him. She believed every word I said. I knew exactly what she was about to do, and now Mike will get to experience the so-called justice Julie is about to dish out.

As I'm hovering above Mike's body, I'm observing Julie's behavior. She carries herself calmly and determinedly, but she's about to be in for a rude awakening. I can see the hate and anger boil deep inside her. Her anticipation for revenge is to the max, and it's only a matter of time before she does the deed.

She stands up over Mike's body and grips the gardening shears tightly. I watch her gleam down at Mike with her hateful eyes. She wastes no time pulling down Mike's pants and underwear. Oh, how funny this is! It looks like Mike's unconscious mind is enjoying being tied up. His unconscious being is probably dreaming of his fantasy. He's about to face the reality that this is no fantasy as soon as he becomes conscious.

Julie aligned the shears right in between Mike's semi-hard erection, and with a quick, swift motion, she closes the handle to the tool. Suddenly, Mike screams and cries out. Look who's finally awake. I watch as the blood squirts out of the wound. In no time, the bed starts to get soaked in a dark red. I notice immediately after the decapitation, Julie keels over and vomits all over the floor. I then hear Mike cry out to Julie why she did what she did, through pain-gritted teeth.

Julie immediately burst out in tears. I feel as if she noticed the change of tone in Mike's voice. Mike sounded more like Mike than when I controlled his mind. Julie threw her hands to her face, letting out the most horrible hiccuping sobs I've ever heard. She exclaims the fact that she's starting to realize that it's her actual boyfriend again.

I'm hovering, listening to her go on about the fact that I told her it would never be possible for Mike's actual mind to return to him. This only confused the pain-wracked Mike. He is so confused and has no idea what she is saying. I'm listening to Julie try and explain her situation to him and I'm just getting bored. This part sucks!

I turn my attention to the blood pouring out of Mike's body. What a lovely sight. I can't wait to find my next mind to take over so I can feel that feeling of causing pain and hurt to someone. Mike has lost a lot of blood, and I can tell that he doesn't have much longer left to live. I got excited over that fact. It didn't take long for Mike's face to turn very pale and his lips a bluish color.

The two sat there debating and explaining that they lost track of the time. It was too late to save Mike, based on how much blood he's lost. I gain interest in the conversation when Julie started to realize how useless she was once again. I've watched her throw up a couple of times, frozen a few times, and listened to her awful crying. When she realizes that Mike was about to lose his life forever, she became even more hysterical. I love every minute of this. The harsh reality, slapping her across her face. That's what you get for interfering with my plans, you fucking bitch!

I watched them apologize and say their "I love you" and decided it was time for me to move on. I need to find my next mind to control. It's not the end for Julie yet. I must think *about my options smartly. Who could she possibly run into as she's trying to make her escape? Oh, Julie, your night has only begun.*

Chapter Twenty-Eight: Julie

I couldn't move. I'm frozen once again. How am I supposed to shake this state of shock? I kept my head on his chest with my eyes closed. I didn't want to look left or right. If I looked one way I'd see Mike's empty gaze. Lifeless. If I looked the other way, I would see my mistake made from the rage and anger that caused the end of my love. I decided to just keep my eyes closed. It still hurt not looking in either direction, since I could no longer feel or hear his heartbeat. I continued to sob and feel sorry about the situation for a little while longer.

I don't want to move and face the reality that he's truly gone. I already miss him. I need to get out of here. Far away. I would never get the chance to see my love again and will have to live with the fact that he's no longer with me. How am I supposed to explain this to anyone? What am I supposed to do? Am I supposed to return home, go back to classes and pretend everything is fine? I'm not going to be able to function. I wouldn't even know how to explain this. The police will probably find me guilty and send me away. I mean, I am guilty. I'm the reason why he's dead.

I shook my head, trying to clear my mind from all the questions and thoughts that are swimming around. What if I just disappeared? I don't even know how I can put the blame on someone who's not even here. If anyone investigated the doctor, they'd find out he "died" years ago and find me just insane. Am I insane? I need to go find somewhere to lie low and figure out what I should do next. I can't stay here just in case someone does stumble across all the dead bodies now that they're starting to pile up. Someone will soon come out and investigate what's going on, I'm sure.

I remembered that I have the car keys in my pocket. I reached down to my pockets and patted them just to make sure. They were still there. I felt them dig into my leg as I patted each pocket. I'll take the car, find a nearby hotel and crash there for the night so I can refocus my mind and figure out my next moves.

I went over to the closet and grabbed a sheet from the shelf. I walked slowly back to Mike and once again looked down at him.

"I'm so sorry, Mike." I spoke softly. "I love you."

I held back my sobs and placed the sheet over his body. I didn't want him to be left uncovered like that. After I covered him up with the sheet, I placed my hand on his chest one last time, feeling the emptiness where a heartbeat should be. One last glance and I started moving towards the door to the room.

I slowly made my way down the stairs. The emotions I'm feeling are all over the place. My legs feel weak. My body feels heavy, and my mind is a blur. I remembered leaving my phone in the kitchen to charge last night. I made my way to the kitchen to grab it. As I entered the kitchen, I picked up the phone and saw that I had no notifications. That was a good thing, because I didn't want to speak to anyone. I want to confide in someone so bad, but I don't know what I would say to anyone.

I slipped the phone into my pocket and moved towards the closet in the hall by the door. I'm going to grab a jacket this time. I'm not going to be cold from the cool breeze that's out there. As I put the jacket on, I paused for a moment to see if I had everything that I would need for the time being. I have the car keys in my pocket, my phone, and a jacket, and I grabbed a flashlight just in case. I nodded to myself, satisfied that I was ready to finally leave the cabin.

I opened the front door and immediately felt the cool breeze come across my face. It was a smart idea to wear a jacket. I'm sure once the sun comes out, it'll heat back up just a bit and it'll feel comfortable again. I made my way over to the car and unlocked it. I slid into the seat and placed the flashlight down on the passenger seat. I started up the car and turned on the heat just a little bit to counteract the coolness from outside. I'm such a freeze-baby. I hate the cold even if it's a cool night like tonight.

When the car is started and I have the temperature just right, I begin heading down the drive towards the main road. It was very dark outside with hardly any lights on the street. The only means of light was coming from the car and the headlight on this car isn't the best. It's a good thing that I'm wired. My emotions and adrenaline are keeping me wide awake, even though I've had hardly any sleep.

I continued down the long drive, staring into the deep darkness, pondering exactly what I should do next. I finally made it out of the drive and turned into the main road heading away from the cabin for good. The surroundings on this road seemed even darker than the drive headed away from the cabin.

I continued down the road for a few miles, seeing nothing along the way. The quiet was starting to kill me. The quiet was accelerating my reckless mind that continued to race a mile a minute. I reached to turn on the radio to try and distract my burning mind until I felt something wrong with the car. I heard a popping noise and immediately thought it was a tire. Shit. Did I run something over? This is the last thing that I need right now. I haven't made it far from the cabin, but I'm far enough away from a hotel. It's late at night and it's cold out. I'm all alone on top of everything.

I unbuckled my seatbelt and opened the door to step outside. I walked around the car to the front to check on the front tires. They were both losing air at a rapid pace. Damn, I must have run something over. What would do this much damage though? Both tires? I didn't notice anything in the road. Or maybe I did and didn't recognize it. It is dark out here and I have a hard time just looking in front of me.

I stood there staring in disbelief. Great I have something else to add to my plate right now. What am I going to do now? Everyone that I know lives out of state and I really don't want to call the police. At all. Maybe I can see if I can look up a tow company on my phone. I could call them to come help me out. Get the car worked on while I stay somewhere nearby to collect my thoughts.

I made my way back to the driver side of the car and climbed back inside. I sat in the seat and closed the door. I turned up the heat just a little bit more and grabbed my phone. I attempted to open the internet app on my cell phone, but it wouldn't connect. Shit. Of course there's no service out here. What the fuck do I do now? I placed my head into my hands and closed my eyes. This day is getting worse, not getting any better. It can't get any worse than it is right now. Right?

Through my closed eyes I sensed the sky getting brighter. I opened my eyes and couldn't believe what I was seeing. A vehicle was approaching my car. I was both relieved and afraid. What if it were a police cruiser headed towards me? How will I explain what's going on? As the vehicle got closer, I could faintly make out that it was a tow truck. Theres no way that I just got this lucky. Sure enough, I can see the lights on top of the truck with all its equipment hooked up in the back. The truck stopped right beside my car, and I can finally make out the name on the side of the truck. It read: **Lou's**.

I wonder if it's the same guy from the store when we first came up here. I didn't get to meet the man in the store when we were there. Only Mike went inside, but he said that the man looked creepy as fuck. The truck does look familiar now that it's in full view. The driver rolled his window down and I did the same. The man in the truck indeed looks creepy as fuck. He smiled politely to me, but his teeth were yellow, well, what was left, that is.

"Hello ma'am." He said politely. "Are you okay?"

"Hello sir." I responded expressing the same amount of politeness. "Unfortunately, no. I must have run something over in the road. Both my tires have a flat."

"My." He said peering down at the tires. "Seems like you are in a bit of a bind."

"I don't have any service out here either." I said almost quietly.

"I can always tow it to my shop." He offered. "And then we can figure out where you can stay in the meantime. I should have it fixed by the end of tomorrow if that works for you."

"That would be much appreciated." I said gratefully.

I watched as he moved his truck in front of mine and lined up his equipment to hook up the car. After he signaled that the car was properly hooked up, he walked over to my driver's side window. I rolled down the window once more to see what he needed.

"It'll be safer if you sit up next to me in the truck." He said sympathetically. "Just in case anything happens to the car on the way to my shop."

"Yeah, okay." I said gingerly.

I climbed out of the car and closed the door. I followed the man to his truck and climbed into his passenger seat.

"It shouldn't take long to get to my shop." He began. "It's about 20 minutes down this road."

"This is going to be the longest 20 minutes," I thought to myself. I just need to get these tiers fixed and a place to collect my thoughts. I really need to figure out what my next steps are going to be.

"I'm Lou." He said, glancing over to me. "I was already on my way back to my shop when I saw your car and figured you might need help."

"I'm very lucky that you were around." I said, trying not to look at him. "I thought for sure I would be screwed. I'm Julie."

"It's nice to meet you, Julie." He said, giving off that ugly smile.

God, the smell in this truck is unbearable. He gives off the stench of someone who hasn't had a shower in weeks. The stench of stale cigarettes flowed through the truck. His clothes were torn and covered in stains. Mike was right about this guy; he is a creepy, disgusting man. I'm just glad he was kind enough to help me out.

"Do you mind if I crack a window?" I asked him to try not to gag on the smell surrounding me.

"Of course not." He said agreeing. "Whatever makes you comfortable."

"Thank you." I said gratefully.

I rolled down the window manually, since this truck is an older model. I didn't mind since I could get fresh air finally. I would do anything to not inhale this awful stench. For a little while I stared out my window. There was not much to look at, but it was better than trying to have a conversation with Lou. My mind was racing anyways. So much is going through my mind now. I can't pinpoint one idea from the next. I wonder how much further we must go.

"What were you doing out here this late at night?" He asked.

"I couldn't sleep, so I thought a drive would be nice." I lied.

"Are you not with that group of kids I saw at the shop a couple days ago?" He pried.

"Yes, we stopped for gas on the way to the cabin." I spoke.

"I do recognize this car." He continued. "Is this your boyfriend's car then?"

"It is." I stated.

"And where is your boyfriend then?" He asked as if he noticed something isn't right. "You want me to drop you off at the cabin before I take the car to the shop?"

Damnit. What do I do now? He's asking a ton of fucking questions. I guess I would too if I were him. I really wish he wouldn't have asked so many questions. If I tell him no, then he would continue to ask more questions. If I tell him yes, then I'm back to where I started with no means of escaping. If I tell him yes, he might ask to take me to the door to make sure I'm safe. Maybe it wouldn't be such a bad thing. I doubt the old man would go any further than the entrance to the cabin. Mike is up the stairs and not in the open.

"If you're worried about how to get the car when I finish working on it, don't. I'll tow it back to you when it's finished, unless you have another vehicle there." He said when I didn't respond the first time.

"That would be great." I responded nervously. "We don't have another vehicle, so dropping it back off would be very nice of you."

"Since you kids are out of town, I won't charge you for the tow." He offered. "We will discuss some kind of payment tomorrow."

"You are too generous." I said, showing appreciation.

One thing after the other. I just keep getting put into situations to worry about. I can't focus on the first thing when other situations pop up. Now I must worry about what happens right now before I get to worry about how the hell I'm going to proceed after this. I need to get far away from this cabin. Now I won't even have a car. I must worry about Lou finding out that all my friends are missing. Well, I mean "dead," but hopefully he won't piece that together.

I recognized the driveway as we approached it. We were beginning to head down towards the cabin. This fucking sucks. My anxiety was at an all-time high once more. We strolled down the long, endless drive.

"We're almost to the cabin now." He pointed out. "I wish you the best if your boyfriend asks where the car is."

He gave off a chuckle, followed by a nasty cough. I was slightly relieved. This must mean that he intends to just drop me off without trying to walk me inside. That would solve this slight problem. I could focus on the next problem if that is the case. We neared the front of the cabin finally. The sheer moments of awkwardness were finally coming to an end.

"All right." He said, looking over to me. "Here we are. I'll try to hurry with the car and have it back to you tomorrow. Try and get some sleep."

"Thank you so much." I said to him, managing a smile on my face. "I appreciate all that you've done for me tonight and all that you're continuing to do."

I gave him one last smile and grabbed the door handle to open the door. I almost hurriedly climbed out of the truck as fast as possible without looking too suspicious. I shut the door to the truck and headed to the front door of the cabin. Once I reached the front door, I opened it and stepped inside. I immediately went to the window by the door to peer out it. I cautiously waited and watched as Lou's truck finally went back down the drive out of sight.

I let out a deep breath. A rush of relief leaving my body. Now that he's gone and didn't ask anymore questions or to come inside, it left me feeling very lucky that he was around. There were no police here either, not that there should be, but I'm still glad that there wasn't. Mike is still lying upstairs dead. I have a feeling that there isn't a killer around any longer. Maybe it was Mike the entire time and I was just being led to believe a deep lie. I'm not entirely sure what to think right now or where to start. For the moment, I felt a sense of security. I feel as if I'm safe to give myself some time to think about what my next move should be. For some reason though, something feels off. I can't place it exactly, but there's a feeling in my gut that's not good.

Chapter Twenty-Nine: Julie

I continued to lean on the front door. I couldn't shake the feeling of something not being right. It must be just my anxiety. My mind has been working overtime as of late. Now is the time to sit and think about what I should do next. The first order of business is figuring out if I should continue to stay here and wait for the car to get dropped back off. That would be the smartest option; that way I have means of transportation. If I take that option, I will have to make sure I would be able to get rid of Lou quickly. Not only would I have to get rid of him quickly, but in the meantime I would have to worry about the police coming around. I still feel like I don't have to worry about them as much as I think, but with Frank missing as well, I'm sure someone would soon start asking questions.

I moved into the living area and sat down on the couch. I started to rock back and forth and put my head in between my hands. I can't slow down my mind. The options are weighing on me. I don't want to do this alone. I still can't believe that I survived this horror. Now I just must wait for the consequences. There's a possibility that all of this will fall on me. I'm left with the scraps and the fault. No one will ever believe my side of the story. I mean, how can I blame someone? It all sounds so crazy.

Even though I shouldn't, I feel like I need a drink. Maybe a drink will calm me down just a bit. Enough for me to focus my mind. I walked over to the bar cart over in the corner and picked up a wineglass. I opened a bottle of red and poured myself a glass. The first sips of the wine went down, leaving a slight burn as all the notes of the wine explored my taste buds. The second sip went down a lot easier as I enjoyed the taste. Before I decided to sit back down, I picked up my bottle and then returned to my seat. I continued to sip on the wine. My body started to warm up and my head started to calm down.

I have no clue how I will proceed with my life. Tears formed in my eyes as I kept running scenarios through my mind. People at school will notice that I'm the only one that made it back from vacation. Three missing. There is no way I can make something up when there are three missing. If I went to the police on my own to explain everything that happened, I wouldn't have any proof of my story. Especially when most of it is just a campfire story. They wouldn't believe me and would put all three murders on me. I'd be sent to jail for all the murders. All the parents would be so devastated. I feel so bad for them. They will never believe the reality of what just happened, let alone suspect that I had a mental break and went completely crazy.

I took another sip of the wine. The wine in the glass was almost empty, and yet I hadn't come up with a solid plan of action. Every path that I could think of ends up poorly. If I decided to not return home, that would create questions about where I am. It'll make me look guilty for running. Then there would be four of us not returning to school. Once they find me, my story will be less believable than what it already was.

I poured myself another glass of wine. The one glass wasn't enough. I still have no idea what the Hell to do. I'm feeling the effects from the wine. I heard a noise coming from outside the window in the room. I snapped out of my deep thought and listened carefully. Maybe it was just an animal. I got up from my seat and headed towards the window. I looked outside and didn't see anything. There was no movement out there.

I heard a sound coming from outside in the other room as well. Man, I'm really losing my mind. The sound came once more. This time I jumped at the sound. A chill ran down my spine and I shook it off. I moved towards the sound in the other room cautiously. I looked out the window and again, I saw nothing. I'm not sure if my anxiety or the wine is making me paranoid, but that feeling in my gut has returned once more. Something feels off. I'm getting a bad vibe, a bad kind of energy that keeps looming around.

I jumped once more when I heard a crashing sound come from the kitchen. It almost sounded like glass shattering. This time, I became scared. I went back over to the fireplace and picked up the fire poker. My safety net. It got me out of a bind once already. I walked over to the end table by the couch and picked up the flashlight. I'm not going to navigate the house in the dark.

I carefully made my way to the kitchen, pointing the flashlight down on the floor as I walked. I listened to my surroundings carefully, trying to hear any other noise coming from the kitchen. The house remained silent. The last noise I heard was from the kitchen. I placed my back against the wall, heading into the kitchen and controlled my breathing. I kept the flashlight pointing downward and prepared myself to peek around the corner. After a moment, I peered around the corner. I didn't see anything initially. I shone the light into the kitchen and scanned the area. There was no sign of anyone in the room.

I turned the corner when I noticed no one was in the room. I shone the light around the room and didn't notice anything disturbed. The sound sounded like glass shattering, so I pointed the light at the kitchen windows. They were still intact. I moved towards the back door and checked it. The glass to the door was shattered in the middle area of the door. I examined the floor surrounding the back door and noticed the glass on the ground. Surrounding the glass was a brick that seemed like the cause of the breakage. I peered out the window and came up empty once again. I flashed the light to the backyard of the cabin and scanned the surrounding area. There was no one out there.

My senses are now extreme. There's someone out there messing with me. I'm sure of it. Multiple noises and now this shattered window. Someone threw this brick through it, but why? They didn't enter the cabin. I have no idea who it could be. There's no one out here. It seems like someone is trying to send me a message. Almost as if they are warning me that they knew what I've done.

As I'm still scanning the yard, I hear a thump come from upstairs. I immediately glance straight up at the ceiling towards the noise. My eyes grow large from the idea that someone was moving around upstairs. Mike is dead. There is no way it's him moving around. Did someone throw this stone through the window as a distraction to find their way upstairs? How would they get in up there? I guess I didn't bother checking to see if the windows are locked. As soon as I came back to the cabin, I stayed downstairs. I didn't want to be anywhere near Mike when I came back.

Another thump came from upstairs. This time I was able to pinpoint the sound. It was coming from my room. My head started to swim in thoughts. He's dead. He's dead. It can't be Mike. There is no way it's him. He wasn't breathing when I left. I haven't seen anyone outside the entire time. There was no car that made its way up the drive. Anything is possible after the events that have happened as of late.

I took a deep breath; I have no interest in going upstairs. Can't this fucking nightmare just come to an end already? I slowly headed towards the stairs. My heartbeat is racing out of my chest. I shone the light on the floor as I walked towards the steps. I took a quick peak up the stairs and didn't see anything. I didn't flash the light to the top of the staircase, because I don't want whoever is up there to see me coming. I listened carefully to any sound of movement, but there was nothing but silence.

I took each step with extreme caution. I kept the light down on the stairs without pointing it up. I was in no hurry to make it to the top. I continued to listen to my surroundings the higher I got on the stairs. I made it to the top ledge and made my way down the hall. I once again placed my back to the wall near the doorway to the room. I gripped the fire poker tightly as I tried to continue to control my breathing. I peered around the corner quickly to investigate the room. I didn't see any movement in the room, and I was able to make out that Mike was still lying on the bed.

I slowly entered the room and flashed the light throughout the bedroom. It was empty besides the sight of Mike on the bed. At least today wasn't going to be crazy enough to have a dead body walking around. What was the source of the sounds coming from up here? Since the last sound, there hasn't been a peep since. I opened the closet and there was nothing there. I checked under the bed and found nothing. I made my way to the bathroom and first pushed the door towards the wall. There was nothing behind it. I quickly opened the shower curtain and found nothing there either.

I shook my head at the thought that this is the exact scenario I was in earlier when I was trying to get the jump on Mike. This is ridiculous. Maybe I am turning into a crazed individual. I decided to check the rest of the rooms up here just to make sure. After I was done with the search, I came up empty. I just don't understand. All the windows are shut and locked. It didn't look like anyone broke in up here. There was no sign of anyone outside. All there was, was the broken window to the kitchen door. Maybe someone was trying to just leave me a message. But who? That seems to be the question of the night. Maybe it was some neighborhood kids up to no good. I have no idea. I am extremely frightened and don't want to be here any longer.

On my way back down the stairs, I decided that I will check the doors and windows one more time to make sure they're locked. I looked around both yards and didn't see anything moving. I made my way back to the living room and just decided to pour myself another glass of wine. I sat down on the couch and sipped on the alcoholic beverage. I shook my head in frustration. I'm mentally exhausted at this point. I want to be in my bed at home, curled up in a ball.

My eyes began to feel heavy. The wine is starting to take its effects and I no longer care about anything. Maybe if I sleep the time will pass by and I can get the car back. The rest will sort itself out, I'm sure. There haven't been more sounds throughout the cabin. On top of the wine working its magic the peace and quiet were starting to make me extremely tired. I rested my head on the back of the couch and before I knew it, I was out like a light.

Chapter Thirty: Dr. Jacob Underwood

I took my happy ass in search of my next mind to control. I need someone stupid but capable. I still have a loose end to attend to. I don't let my victims escape my clutches. I journeyed down the road in hope of finding my next poor soul.

Just down the road, I came across a truck parked off to the side. When I got closer, I noticed it was a tow truck. Oh, this might be too perfect. I can use this as bait and patently get the trust from Julie. Hopefully her mind is too fried to put up a fight. When I got closer, I noticed it was a tow truck. The name on the side of the truck was worn but readable. It read: **Lou's.** *This must be the truck from the filler station not far from the cabin.*

When I finally saw the man, he did look familiar. It was hard to not recognize the horrid look of the man. He looked awful. Truly creepy. I love the look. He surely will do. I watched as he spit in his cup. A nasty habit. The cup was almost filled with the dark brownish-black tobacco spit. He was busy looking at some magazine. I took a closer look and noticed it was a dirty magazine. He was sitting in his truck, parked on the side of the road, looking at a dirty magazine. What a sick bastard. I also noticed that his pants were unbuttoned as well. This man will do the trick.

His mind will do. I will use this vessel to get what I want. This time I will be successful, and she will not escape my clutches.

Chapter Thirty-One: "Lou"

I pulled over at my usual spot. I just finished doing my usual errands for the day, so I finally came to my special spot before I head back to the shop. I come here every evening to destress from the day and to look at my magazines while I enjoy a big dip. Nothing special about it, but it gets me relaxed before I must return to the shop to do my closing work.

Today I felt like there were eyes on me though. I have this weird feeling. No one is ever around at this time of the night. Everyone is inside, having supper and bunkering down from this killer on the loose. It's nice for me, since I get to have my alone time on the road. Today just seemed different. I looked around and didn't notice anything unusual. I spit into my cup and continue looking at my magazine. God, these women in the magazines are so heavenly. I would do anything for a night with one of these goddesses.

Out of nowhere, my head started to hurt. I felt like I was having a real bad headache. I pinched my eyes closed and rubbed my face. When I opened my eyes, the pages of the magazine became blurry. Everything started to spin. Everything went dark.

Finally. I opened my eyes and saw the world through Lou's eyes. God. This man is distasteful. Absolutely disgusting. I'm going to go off on a whim and assume Julie will try and drive away from the cabin now that Mike is dead. I'll set up some spike strips in the road. The area is dark, so she won't see them. She probably won't even pay attention to the road anyway with everything on her mind.

I backed out of the spot Lou was held up at and headed towards the cabin. Once I got close to the cabin, I stopped the truck and stepped out. I went to the back of the truck and pulled out the road spikes. I have absolutely no idea why Lou had them in his truck, but in my assumption, he was probably planning on doing this to someone eventually. This isn't the standard equipment a tow truck carries.

Without a second thought on the matter, I took the spikes and laid them out on the road. Such a perfect spot for them. It's pitch black here. Not even the headlights on the car could spot them. All I would have to do is drive down the road a little, enough so I can still see the car coming, and then go to the rescue. I really hope that it'll be Julie that hits the spike and no one else. I seriously doubt it'll be someone else; usually no one is out here around this time of the night. I also hope that my gut is right and she's planning on running away from the cabin.

I climbed back into the truck to head back down the road. I turned around to head back down the road, after I got a little way away from the spikes, I pulled the car into a U-turn to face the right direction again. All I must do now is wait patiently to see if my trap works or not. All I have is time, so being patient won't be difficult for me.

After what seemed like an hour or so that passed by, I saw headlights headed my way. Here we go, I thought to myself. This is it. The moment that I've been waiting for. I kept the lights off on the truck and put it into reverse. I backed up for about a mile. Easy work since no one is around. I'm going to wait a few more minutes before I decide to come to the rescue.

A few minutes passed by, and I felt like it was a decent time to go check out my trap. I started the truck back up and turned on my lights. I headed down the road closer to the trap. From the distance, I could tell it was Mike's car off on the side of the road. Yes. My plan worked. Well, step one of my plan worked.

I slowed the truck down as I approached Mike's car. I pulled up to the driver's side window and rolled my window down. I saw Julie sitting in the driver's seat and looking nervous at first. She then rolled down her window.

"Hello, Ma'am." I said, trying to sound as polite as possible. "Are you okay?"

"Hello sir." She responded sounding respectful. "Unfortunately, no. I must have run something over in the road. Both my tires have a flat."

"My." I said, pretending to pay attention to her tires, even though I knew exactly what the problem was. "Seems like you are in a bit of a bind."

"I don't have any service out here either." She said in almost a whisper.

Pretty stupid to say to someone, especially at a time like this with no one around. Not able to call for help. Not like she has anyone to call anyway. Ha. Ha.

"I can always tow it to my shop." I offered, as if I gave a flying fuck. "And then we can figure out where you can stay in the meantime. I should have it fixed by the end of tomorrow if that works for you."

"That would be much appreciated." She responded, sounding grateful.

I moved the truck to tow the car. I aligned the tow to the car's fender. I stepped out of the truck to hook up the car to the tow. After I secured the car to the tow truck, I walked over to Julie. She still had her window rolled down.

"It'll be safer if you sit up next to me in the truck." I tried to sound sympathetic. "Just in case anything happens to the car on the way to the shop."

"Yeah, Okay." She said, almost hesitantly.

She got out of the car and headed to the passenger side of the truck. I walked with her to myside. We got into the truck at the same time. I could tell she didn't really want to get into the truck with me, but she didn't have any other choice.

"It shouldn't take long to get to my shop." I said, looking at her. "It's about 20 minutes down this road."

I glanced over and noticed that she was looking out the window. I could only imagine what's going through her mind in this moment. She probably didn't plan on this happening. Hell, I don't even know what exactly she was planning on doing. Where was she planning on going? How would she explain anything to anyone? I am very interested in finding out. Eventually, I will find out what her plan was, if she even had one.

"I'm Lou." I lied, looking over to her. "I was already on my way to my shop when I saw your car and figured you might need help."

"I'm very lucky that you were around." She said, still looking out the passenger window and then the front window.

It seems as if she's doing everything to avoid looking at me. Honestly, I don't blame her. Lou is one ugly son of a bitch. "I thought for sure I would be screwed. I'm Julie."

She's not screwed yet. She thinks this is going to be the highlight of her night. She's in for one hell of a night.

"It's nice to meet you, Julie." I said, giving her one of Lou's awful smiles. I love it. The smile is so hideous; it's making her very uncomfortable. I'm going to use that to my advantage later. Make her do crazy things to the disgusting old man. This body smells awful.

"Do you mind if I crack a window?" She asked me, as she was trying to hide the fact that she couldn't take the stench any longer.

"Of course not." I said as politely as possible. "Whatever makes you comfortable."

"Thank you." She responded, showing the same amount of respect.

I periodically glanced over, watching her as she rolled the window down. I could see the sense of relief coming off her. She glared out her window for a while during the drive. It was silent for a while. She had this puzzling, confused face as she glared out the window.

"What were you doing out here this late at night?" I finally asked, breaking the silence.

"I couldn't sleep, so I thought a drive would be nice." She said. I can clearly tell that she's lying. Even so, I already know it's a lie.

"Are you not with that group of kids I saw at the shop a couple days ago?" I asked her, already knowing the answer.

"Yes, we stopped for gas on the way to the cabin." She answered.

"I do recognize this car." I stated. "Is this your boyfriend's car then?"

"It is." She replied.

"And where is your boyfriend then?" I asked, trying not to grin at the image of him dead on the bed. "You want me to drop you off at the cabin before I take the car to the shop?"

She was quiet for a long moment. Seems like she's trying to sort out her lies. I'm going to let her think about how she should answer for a minute. I enjoy this game.

"If you're worried about how to get the car when I finish working on it, don't. I'll tow it back to you when it's finished, unless you have another vehicle there." I said, finally breaking the silence. I've given her enough time to think of her responses.

"That would be great." She said nervously, sensing that I had noticed the stall between responses. "We don't have another vehicle, so dropping it back off would be very nice of you."

"Since you kids are out of town, I won't charge you for the tow." I offered her, trying to relax her and completely gain her trust. "We will discuss some kind of payment tomorrow."

"You are too generous." She said gratefully. Seems like I have gained her trust. At least for now anyways.

"We're almost to the cabin now." I said as we were coming close to the driveway to the cabin. "I wish you the best if your boyfriend asks where the car is."

I saw her give off a shy grin as she looked at me for the first time in a long while. The smile didn't last long as she remembered how repulsive I looked.

"All right." I said, looking at her. "Here we are. I'll hurry with the car and have it back to you tomorrow. Try and get some sleep."

"Thank you so much." She said humbly. "I appreciate all that you've done for me tonight and all that you're continuing to do."

She gave me one last awful attempt at a smile as she reached for the door handle. I can tell that she was in a hurry to get out of the truck, even though she tried her best to not be obvious about it. I continued to watch her walk away from the truck and towards the front door. I sat and waited for her to open the door and go inside. Hopefully, it'll show her that I'm trying to be a gentleman, making sure she makes it inside safely. She opened the door and closed it quickly. I can see that she went straight to the window to see what I was about to do. Once she got to the window, I put the truck in reverse to navigate my way to turn around in their drive.

I headed back down the driveway away from the cabin to the main road once again. I turned right instead of left towards the shop. I'm going to drive down a little way and pull off for a few minutes. I'm going to give her some time to think and to feel safe once again. Once there's been enough time for her to feel safe, I will continue my fun. I'm going to take my time once I finally get my hands on her.

I've waited too damn long to play with this one. She's stubborn and resourceful. Toughest victim I've encountered so far. She already killed off my last vessel. It won't happen a second time. I know her tricks. I'm hoping that her mind is too far gone to be as smart as she has been thus far.

All I must do now is sit and wait. The time to make my move will soon approach.

Chapter Thirty-Two: "Lou"

I've waited long enough for Julie to contemplate what she will do with her life from here on out. I climbed out of the truck and started the long, but short, walk to the cabin. I closed the door to the truck and headed down the road. I can't wait to start fucking with her. I'm going to take my time messing with her. I'll get into her head first. Not like I already got in there. I'll make sure she really feels crazy. She probably feels so hopeless right now. What is she going to do if I just let her go back to her old life? How would she explain what's going on?

The night was quiet, with only the noise coming from the nocturnal animals lurking about in the shadows. The sway of the leaves is making that eerie noise that I love so much. There isn't anyone else out on the streets. I haven't seen anyone in a very long time other than Julie, when I made her car break down. The night air was brisk. I love this kind of weather. It's not too cold or unbearably hot. I hate chasing victims in the heat. The slight breeze was just enough for me to be comfortable.

I finally made it to the drive leading up to the cabin. In the distance I can see a light on in the living room. She must be sitting downstairs. I wouldn't blame her for not wanting to be upstairs with the dead body. I picked up my pace slightly; the anticipation was getting to me. I made sure I remained as quiet as possible till it was time for me to finally make a noise.

I slowed my pace down as I neared the front yard. I'm going to use the shadows for cover just to make sure I'm not caught. If I get caught, my fun will be over before it even begins. I silently crept up to the front of the cabin. I moved towards the windows and peered inside. I can see Julie over by their bar cart. It looks like she's about to open a bottle of wine. After she got the bottle opened, I watched her grab a glass and pour herself some. She took a long sip from the glass and could see that she shook her head after it. She's probably feeling that first warm, flavorful burst from the notes in the wine. I watched her then walk to the couch to have a seat. She took another sip of the wine. It almost looks like she's starting to relax. I can't have that. Maybe a little mysterious noise from outside will jump-start that heart of hers once again.

I reached down and picked up one of the stones lying around the flower bed in the front below the window. When I got the stone in my hand, I trained my aim, pointing towards the trash cans that are next to the driveway. I threw the stone and managed to hit the aluminum can. It made a loud, ringing bang sound. Perfect. That should get her attention.

I saw her turn her head towards the sound. When she made the move to get up from the couch, I moved towards the side of the cabin. There were windows on the side of the cabin as well and I paused so I could look through the window to watch what she would do. I watched her cautiously move towards the front window. She slowly looked out the window, scanning the yard to see if she could find what made the sound. She shook her head after finding nothing in her view. She scanned the outside surroundings once more, then turned around.

Time to make another sound. This time from this side of the building. What can I use this time? I looked around in search for something that would make a loud enough noise. I saw a garden shovel leaning up against the siding. That will be perfect to use. I picked it up and smacked it against the cabin. The loud clack sound pierced the air. Loud enough to hear from inside. I watched her jump a little from the noise.

She started heading this way and I hurriedly, but cautiously, moved away from my spot. I made my way to the back of the cabin towards the kitchen area. I'm going to give her a moment to look around at the surroundings. It sucks that I can't see her disappointed look. Even more pissed, I won't be able to see her confused, scared look. I then decided this time I'm going to throw something through the back door. Make it seem like someone broke in. That should really get under her skin. Especially when she finds nothing but the broken window on the door.

I searched my surroundings once again and noticed a pile of bricks by the fire pit in the backyard. Yes. Perfect. I'm getting lucky with shit to use around here. Almost like it was meant to be to fuck with her. I moved towards the fire pit and picked up one of the bricks. After I throw this, I'm going to hide behind the bush that's close by. I get to watch her movements this time and don't want to miss her reactions.

I aimed and pointed towards the back door. I carefully threw the brick at the door. A loud crashing sound filled the air. Wow! My aim is on point tonight. First try with the trash can and now with the door, I'm on fire. I quickly moved behind the bush after the brick landed through the door.

The bush is perfect. It was big enough and thick enough to hide my body from sight. I was still able to look through it to see the kitchen. I crouched behind the bush waiting as patiently as I possibly could. The anticipation was starting to get to me, and I was starting to lose the patience I had. After a few moments, I saw what looked like a light from a flashlight flash through the windows. Maybe she went to grab a flashlight to make her feel a bit safer. Oh, how I can picture her slowly walk through the house towards the kitchen expecting someone breaking in.

Another moment passed, and I could see that Julie was finally in the kitchen. The light from the flashlight was still present, as it was flashing around crazily. I watched her walk to the back door, bending over to examine the brick lying on the floor. I watched as she checked the door. I didn't bother unlocking it, so it was still locked. She was looking out the back door into the backyard, scanning the yard. She then took the flashlight and shone the light throughout the yard. I can see the faint light from the flashlight dance back and forth throughout the yard. The light wasn't strong enough to illuminate anything. I was perfectly safe behind this bush.

After a few moments, I watched her turn the light off and turn around. She placed her hand on her forehead and walked out of the kitchen. This was killing me. I want to be inside seeing every emotion and action she was portraying. I want her to feel safe and completely crazy before I make my move.

I stayed behind the bush for a few moments before deciding to leave my hiding place. I'm going to find a way to climb to the second floor of the cabin. I want her to think there's someone walking around upstairs. Maybe she'll think Mike is alive and walking around. Oh, how fun that would be.

I'll just make her think there's someone in the house but surprise her in a different way.

I moved quickly around the side of the house to the window so I could peer in and see what she is up to. I headed around the corner and looked through the side window. I saw her standing there with the flashlight in her hand. She had a confused look on her face. I could also tell that she was slightly terrified. She moved towards the front window and shone the flashlight out the window. She was scanning the yard to see if she could see any movement. She was probably checking the perimeter of the house out. This was my opportunity to figure out a way to head to the second floor.

I moved away from the side window. She probably will come to this one next to search for any movement. I headed towards the backyard once again. I'm going to head to the other side of the house and see if there is a way up on that side. When I got to the other side of the house, I paused to look around. There was one of those flower-ladder-type things leading all the way up the house to a window. Just like in the movies. Except in every movie, the ladder is white with vines tangled up in it. This one was made of wood and looked like it was never used since the place was built. I have no idea if it's even sturdy enough to hold my weight.

The only thing that this ladder had in common with the ones in the movies was that it was completely covered in vines. The vines were overgrown and covered most of the ladder. It was hard to make out the steps on it, and it was hidden well against the siding of the building. This could be my only outlet though, so it must be good enough. I grabbed a hold of the first step that I could grab and placed my foot on the first rung. I could hear the wood creak as I placed my weight on the ladder. Luckily for me, Lou only weighs about a hundred pounds, maybe a buck twenty. Even if this ladder is old and fragile, I should be able to make it all the way up. I just hope that for some reason the window to the room is open. Man, I'd be completely lucky if it were. It would be a sign that this is meant to be.

I continued to climb up the ladder. With each step I can hear the wood creak. It sounded like moans, as if the wood were crying that it was being used. I kept climbing and climbing as the wood held on and held my weight without a fight. I finally made it to the window at the end of the ladder. I tried the window to see if it was unlocked. Indeed, it was. Oh, this is so lovely. I carefully opened the window and climbed in silently. I left the window open so I could climb back out. I'll descend the ladder once I'm done making Julie think there's someone up here.

I stood in the room and realized that this is Mike and Julie's room. There's Mike lying dead on the bed still. What a poor bastard. I quietly laughed. I can't believe that bitch chopped his cick off. Who's truly crazy? Mike, the real Mike never deserved that. He was a great guy. Oops. I fucked him up well. After I stared at Mike for a minute, I trained my ears on the rest of the house. The house was quiet. There was no sound coming from down the stairs. I wonder what she's thinking about in this moment.

When I didn't hear anything and I got bored thinking about what Julie was up to, especially not being able to see her emotions, I decided it was time to make some noise up here. I stomped on the ground a few times, loud enough for her to hear movement coming from the floor up here. I quickly moved towards the hallway and made another stomp in a different area. Maybe she'll think there's someone walking around.

Knowing Julie, she will take her time to investigate the noise, so I had plenty of time to leave the bedroom. I headed back into the room and went straight for the window. I pulled myself out of the window and placed my feet back on the top rung of the ladder. I closed the window before I went back down the ladder. When I made it to the ground level of the cabin, I went to the backyard. I rounded the corner towards the back door. I reached my hand through the broken window and unlocked the door.

Once I made my way inside, I closed the door silently and locked the door. I went to the back room of the kitchen and decided to bunker down and wait a while. I'm sure it'll take Julie quite some time to search the upstairs for an intruder. She's probably up there with some kind of small weapon searching to strike down whoever is in the house. Meanwhile, I'll just be waiting for the perfect opportunity, however long that will take.

I found a place in the dark backroom and crouched down. I trained my ears to listen to the upstairs of the cabin. I can slightly hear her move around room to room. I thought I heard a sigh as she was descending the stairs. I couldn't tell if she was talking to herself or not, but I can imagine she's probably asking herself what the fuck is happening. I can hear her clearly now that she's back downstairs. I heard her come into the kitchen. I carefully peered around the corner. This time she turned the backlight on and observed the surroundings. She looked around for a moment, and when she came up empty, she turned the light back off and left the kitchen.

When she left the kitchen, I got up out of my spot and walked out of the back room into the kitchen. I watched her head back to the living room and walked over to the wall separating the two rooms. I peeked around the corner and watched her head back over to the bar cart. She poured herself another glass of wine. Unbelievable. She's too out of it to be worried about someone fucking with her. She took a sip of the wine and headed back towards the couch. She sat down and continued to drink the wine. She was drinking it a lot quicker than she was earlier. Maybe this is her way of just forgetting the night. It seems like she just doesn't fucking care.

I feel like she's just over the thought of losing her mind. She could be over the fact that her life is about to be shit once she returns home. I peeked around the corner and continued to watch her. She kept pounding the glass of wine, and I could see her head bobbing back and forth as if she were getting tired. She must be fucking exhausted at this point. This will be perfect if she passes out. It'll make my job so much easier.

After a few moments, I watched as Julie's head finally rested on the back of the couch. I can tell that she was out cold. I moved closer to her, still being as silent as possible just in case. The closer I came to Julie, the surer I became that she passed out. I poked her, and she didn't wake up. I clapped my hands loudly and still no response. She must be sleep-deprived from no rest since possibly this morning. Mix the wine on top of it; she'll be in a very deep sleep. It's time to finally have my fun.

Chapter Thirty-Three: Julie

I slowly opened my eyes. Ow. My fucking head hurts. What the fuck. I didn't have that much to drink. I blinked my eyes for a moment and slowly turned my head side-to-side. My vision was slightly blurry. My head is pounding. The room is slightly spinning.

I shook my head slightly to try and come to. When I finally did and the room started to come back to one piece, I realized I was no longer sitting on the couch. What the fuck. Where am I? I scanned the room that I was in to figure out where the hell I was. I came to realize that I was in my room. Mike was still lying on the bed. The room started to smell an awful odor. Stale. The room was very stale and stuffy. There was a musty scent to it. It wasn't unbearable yet, but it would soon get to that point.

How did I end up here? I don't remember coming up here. I was on the couch when I dozed off. I tried to get out of the chair I ended up in but soon realized I couldn't move. I didn't even bother looking at myself. I was too busy scanning my surroundings. My wrists were tied to the chair, and so were my legs. What is going on? Someone was here. How stupid of me to be so careless. I was just so tired and over everything. I wanted to just forget about the situation I was in. I've checked the entire cabin; there was no one here. Everything was silent when I was sitting on the couch.

I wrestled my wrists around, trying to free them. It was hopeless. I couldn't budge them free. I tried kicking my legs free, but I failed at that too. I just want this to end. What did I ever do to deserve this living nightmare? I've never done anything to harm anyone. Ever. Well, besides tonight. I had no choice. I had to.

"Hello, pretty girl." A voice said behind me as I felt a breath on my neck.

"Who, who's there?" I asked, as I gave a shiver as chills ran down my spine.

"It's your savior." The voice continued, this time in my ear.

"Who's there!" I cried out once again.

A man came around from behind me into my view. It was an older man. Wait. No! It was Lou. What the hell is this about?

"Mhmmm." He said looking me up and down. "You smell so nice."

I watched him lick his lips, and I gave a shudder in disgust. This man was so repulsive. I was grateful for his help earlier and obviously blinded by how much of an actual creep he is. It wasn't a coincidence that he was around when I needed help. It was probably planned. The creep probably preys on girls like me all the time. He can't get a female on his own accord, so this is what he does?

"There's something about tight girls like you that just drives me crazy." He said, reaching for a fistful of my hair.

I tried to dodge his hand, moving my head around. He managed to grab my hair and held it tightly as he held my head up, making me look at him. Ugh. He's so fucking gross. He moved his face closer to me. His breath smelled so fucking bad. He gave off that awful smile with his teeth missing. He stuck his tongue out and licked my cheek. I gagged and almost threw up from it.

"Get the fuck off me!" I yelled at him.

"Come on baby." He said, staring at me, smirking. "Let's have some fun."

"You're fucking repulsive!" I cried out.

"I told you we would work out some kind of payment." He said, still giving off that hideous smile. He then looked back over to Mike. "I don't think your boyfriend would mind, after all."

"No!" I continued to cry out. "Let me go! And get the fuck out of here! Keep the fucking car; I don't want it!"

"Maybe we could fuck right next to him." He said, still looking over at Mike.

Tears started to well up in my eyes. I'm in another fucking nightmare, and somehow this one is worse than before. I would rather deal with the doctor who took over Mike's mind than stare at Lou for another moment.

"What do you say, little girl?" He said, moving a finger down my cheek. "He wouldn't mind. I'm sure he would be pleased we invited him to the party."

"You're fucking sick!" I exclaimed.

"Oh, come on." He began to say. "Don't let my age fool you. I'm still hung. And let me tell you, a pretty girl like you gets me nice and hard."

I continued to struggle in the chair I was restrained in. I fought like hell to try and free myself. The restraints were tied very tightly. It was useless, but I tried with all my might.

"Would you rather be somewhere more private? He asked me as he continued to lick his lips. "The feeling of guilt building from getting it from someone other than your boyfriend eating at you? I get that. I can take you into Molly and John's room."

I stopped struggling and looked up at him with a puzzling look.

"How do you know those names?" I asked him.

"It would be ironic since Molly wanted Mike so bad." He continued, ignoring my question. "I could fuck you in their bed for payback for them fooling around behind your back."

"How the fuck do you know their names?!" I asked once more, this time screaming it louder.

"Oh, you stupid bitch." He said, looking down at me. "I know you've missed me very much."

I continued to look up at him with a confused look. His whole demeaner has changed. He sounds confident and calm. He's no longer looking at me like a late-night snack.

"You think I was just going to go away?" He asked. "You thought you would be free of me?"

"Doctor Underwood?" I asked, staring up at him, my eyes getting bigger.

"Did you miss me?" He asked.

"No! That's not possible." I cried out.

"Why?" He asked smiling at me. "Because you killed your boyfriend?"

"I killed him because I thought he was you and no longer himself." I cried out. "You convinced me that his mind would never come back."

"You truly are a stupid girl." He said, continuing to laugh. "I released Mike just before you thought about ending his life."

"How is that possible?" I asked once more.

"I can do whatever I wish." He began. "I no longer held his mind. I wanted him to feel every single moment of what you were about to do to him. I was impressed by your technique. I don't think I would have ever chopped a man's dick off. Ever! Good for you though, taking the situation into your hands and going through with your plan."

"But you said." I started, tears flowing down my cheeks.

"But you said." He stated, mocking me. "I told you what you wanted to hear. I could have released his mind anytime I wanted to."

"Then why didn't you!" I continued to cry out.

"I wasn't done with him yet until you ruined everything." He explained. "You got the better of me that round. It wasn't about to happen again."

"Mike was a better teacher than you think." I explained. "He taught me to survive. Plus, I'm from Texas. I can hold my own."

"Is that right?" He asked me as his smile hasn't gone away. "Look at you now princess."

"I'm exhausted!" I screamed. "I want to be left alone. I've suffered enough."

"I will tell you when you've suffered enough!" He yelled back.

"Just leave me alone!"

"No!" He raised his voice, matching mine.

"Please." I said exhaustedly, tears flowing heavily.

"You don't get to win!" He said angrily. "I'm the one that gets to fucking win!"

I pointed my head down to the floor and just sobbed uncontrollably. I truly am exhausted at this point. I have no will to continue to fight anymore. My life is over. The man that I loved is dead. My best friends are dead. I can't go back home. There will be too many questions. Not enough answers. This fucking nightmare is never going to end. Now look at me. He's got me tied up with no escape.

When I looked back up, I saw him prance around the room through tear-blurred eyes. This fucking guy is beyond crazy. He has no feelings. No regard to anything. It must be nice to be able to control whoever he wants and not feel anything. I almost envy that.

"I need to get you somewhere more comfortable before we start." He said as he continued to dance around the room.

"Continue what?" I asked in almost a whisper.

"Come now." He began to say. "You know exactly what I'm capable of."

I continued to watch him dance around the room. He was full of energy, which looked weird coming from an old man. He moved slowly but swiftly, light on his feet.

"I have an idea." He said as he continued to do his little prance around the bedroom. "I'll take you to the boathouse. You'll feel right at home there. You can die right where your friends have died."

"I would love to see how you'll be able to do that!" I exclaimed, looking up at him. "You chose to control an old man. How are you going to be able to transport my body there? I'm not going to go easily. I'll make it very hard for you to be able to move my body."

"For a smart girl like yourself, you are pretty fucking stupid." He said to me as he stopped prancing around, giving me a more serious look. "Obviously, you wouldn't go out of free will, which is why I will have to knock you the fuck out to take you there."

"You still have to lift my dead-weighted body." I said, feeling a bit of confidence.

"Ha Ha." He laughs at me. "Look at you! You don't weigh much. Trust me, if there's a will, there's a way. I've been waiting a very long time to finally get you onto my table."

I watched him cautiously as he moved away from me and towards the end table by the bed. He reached for something that I couldn't see as his back is turned toward me. He placed whatever it was behind his back as he turned around and headed back over to me. I continued to watch as he moved directly behind me out of my view.

"Just close your eyes." He whispered into my ear. "I'll take great care of you."

As his voice hit my ear, it sent a shiver down the back of my spine, and I gave off a slight shudder. His arm moved around me towards my face, and I could tell there was a rag in his hands. Defenseless, he placed the rag over my nose and mouth. The odor was very potent, and almost immediately I started to lose my ability to see and to be coherent. The odor was the last thing that I remembered.

Chapter Thirty-Four: "Lou"

I watched as her head slowly tilted down. I slid the rag and small bottle of chloroform into my pockets. I moved around the chair to stand in front of Julie. She was out cold. I stood there for a couple minutes just staring at her limp body. It's too bad that I don't find sex a way to get me off. This would be a perfect opportunity to take advantage of her. Probably the best piece of ass Lou has had in a while—or ever, for that matter. It would be great to fuck with her while she's awake to have Lou's body all over her, watching and feeling her squirm around at the horror and disgust. Who knows maybe that would get me off. It would be a form of torture.

I just shook my head and started to loosen her tied-up limbs. I started with one wrist and moved on to the next, then down to her ankles, one at a time. As I managed to get all her restraints from her body, I took a moment and looked at her limp body once more. I reached down to attempt to lift her body. As I went to pick her up, I felt a slightly aggravated pull in the lower back region. Damnit. Julie was right. This old man can't carry her. She looks so easy to move, but this old man does lack the physical aspects that I require.

Luckily for Lou, he contains my mind. My brainpower will overcome this obstacle. Just because he lacks the physical aspect does not mean that this task will be impossible. Hell, I'll even toss her body down the fucking stairs if I need to. There's no time for me to go and find a better candidate for me to control, so Lou will have to do.

I decided to head down the stairs into the main room. There was a large enough rug on the floor that I could use to put her body onto and drag down the stairs. I entered the main room and bent down to grab the rug. Even the rug was slightly heavy for the old man. Damn. What does this dude do? Everything is a fucking workout for him. This is going to take longer than I expected. It would be easier to just do this here, but for one, I don't have all my shit that I want to use, and for two, I've been dying to get Julie onto my table.

I grabbed a corner of the rug and started to drag it towards the stairs. Adrenaline kicked in a bit as I made my way up the stairs and back into the room where Julie's knocked-out body awaits me. As I approached her, I placed the rug down in front of her and took a minute to gather my breathing. I was winded from just doing that. Fuck. This is going to fucking suck.

As I recollected my breathing, I grabbed Julie's arm and tossed her onto the rug. I made sure she was placed evenly on the rug. The rug was big enough to cover her entire body and still have some extra room on it. Once again, I had to catch my breath. Most likely, it was all the years of Lou smoking all his cigarettes that caused him to be so physically useless.

When I finally regained my breath, I reached down and grabbed a corner of the rug once more. I tried to drag her body across the floor, but once again I felt a strain in the lower back region. I let go of the rug and grabbed the area that hurt, wincing as the pain raced across my back. I stood up straight, still rubbing the area that hurt. After a moment, I squatted down and grabbed both ends of the rug. I stood back up and moved toward the door. This time it was a bit easier to drag her body across the floor.

I got to the top of the staircase, trying to figure out how this is going to work. I honestly don't give a shit; I'll just drag her ass down the stairs. The rug should soften the blow from each step. Her head will be pounding when she wakes back up, but that's her problem. My problem is trying to figure out the easiest way to get her down the fucking steps.

I led the way, one step at a time. With each step, I listen to the thud sound that her head makes as it hits each step. I moved slowly down each step. That way it wasn't too much on the old man, and it wasn't too much for Julie's head to take. A few minutes passed by, and I finally made it to the final step. Now all I must do is drag her to the car. Luckily for me, the door is right by the stairs, and the truck is parked not far from the front door. The other thing that I'm lucky for is that we're secluded, so there's no one around to watch me drag a body to the truck.

I continued to drag her body over to the front door. I dropped the rug that I was holding on to and opened the door. I left the door open as I made my way over to the truck. I opened the truck's door; that way it would be one last thing I would have to do. Now all I must do is go back and drag her ass over here and close the doors.

I went back inside and bent down to grab the rug once again. As I had the rug in both my hands, I dragged her out the door and towards the open door to the truck. I rolled her body up in the rug and used all my might and will to hoist her up into the truck. I closed the door to the truck, and before I went to shut the door to the cabin, I stood up straight once again and held my lower back. I waited for my breathing to control itself and for the pain to disappear before I went to shut the cabin's door.

I made my way back to the truck and slowly climbed into the driver's side. I took a moment before I started up the truck. Damn. This is a ton of work, but in the end, it will be worth seeing her stupid, pretty body up on my table. I fired up the truck, listening to the engine purr and sputter. The thought of having enough time to get her onto the table runs through my mind. The chloroform should last till I'm ready to wake her up, but the way this man moves, it's hard to tell.

I backed down the drive and headed to the main road. I headed towards the boathouse. I'm glad the boathouse isn't too far away. And the main door isn't far from where I can park the truck. The hardest part is putting her up on the table. I am not looking forward to that. I continued down the road. The anticipation and the adrenaline start to flow strongly throughout my body. I've waited for this for a while and it's finally happening. I feel as if she'll be a ton of fun up on my table, unlike the others. She puts up a fight and continues to be quite cocky. Unfortunately for her, there's no happy ending. I now have her in my hands. It's the end of the road for her.

I rounded the curve, headed down towards the lake, and parked the truck as close as possible to the boathouse. I turned the truck off and got out. I headed over to the door to the boathouse and checked to see if it was locked. I don't remember locking it after I chased her the last time I was here. Then again, she was the last one here, not me. The door was left unlocked as I reached for the handle. What a bitch. Not locking up after herself.

I left the door wide open and turned to head back to the truck to get Julie. I opened the back door and threw Julie out of the truck onto the floor, still wrapped in the rug, unconscious. I shut the door to the truck, bent down to pick up the ends of the rug and dragged her towards the door to the boathouse.

My breathing was becoming hard and fast as I made my way inside. All I must do now is to get her on top of the table. I gave myself a moment to gather myself and to find the energy and strength to do the final movement. I took a couple of deep breaths, bent down, wrapped my arms around Julie's body, and in a swift motion, I swung her body on top of the table. I winced and groaned at the pain that coursed through my body. Fuck. That took a lot out of me. My breathing was short and fast, and the pain in my back was throbbing.

I wasted no time, though. I placed the restraints on her wrists and ankles, not taking a chance on her waking up. I fully had her secured to the table and decided to take a seat in the chair next to the table. I sat down and watched Julie with hopeful eyes. I can't believe I successfully got her on the table and that she's finally in my grasp to get to work. I'm going to need a bit to gather and collect myself before my fun starts.

As I sat there staring at her, I finally heard her start to come to. Her little moans and groans sent currents throughout my body. The thought of relief flooded over me as I was able to be done by the time she would start to come to. I stayed in my seat and just continued to watch and listen to her.

Chapter Thirty-Five: Julie

I started to slowly open my eyes. They felt heavy and I was a bit dizzy. My vision was blurry and I had a hard time seeing straight. My head was pounding. The pain coursed through me as I continued to blink my eyes open. I winced at the constant throb. Out of reflex, I tried to reach my head to hold it. Of course I couldn't move my hands, and then it dawned on me that I was still being held captive.

I turned my head to the side and scanned the room. I was no longer back in the cabin. Damn. He moved my body. The cold steel seeped through my clothes, and that's when I fully understood exactly where I was. I turned my head in the opposite direction, scanning the room for Lou. I finally spotted him sitting in a chair next to me, just staring at me. He's most likely waiting for me to fully come to.

"Well, look who finally decided to join me." He said as he leaned forward in his chair.

"I see that you managed to get me out here." I replied, looking at him.

"I told you." He began. "If there's a will, there's a way."

"If I'm going to die." I started to say, as I paused to let out a groan from the pounding headache. "Then why don't you give me a little bit of a background on your life? Other than the story I once heard already."

"What good will that do for you?" He asked, puzzled.

"A story just before the fun begins." I played with his ego. "If I'm to die, then what does it matter what you tell me?"

"I usually don't fuck around and tell my prey my life story." He said sternly. "Although old Lou could use a break. I want to be able to savor this, so a little intermission before the leading acts won't hurt."

"I'm just curious as to what made you the way you are." I state, still looking at him. "There's got to be a reason behind all this hate from an early age."

"I don't know who better to talk about, other than myself anyways." He laughs as he sits back all the way in the chair once again. "It's not like you're going anywhere anyway."

That's where he's wrong. I don't give a damn about his poor little traumatic childhood. I knew that he wouldn't be able to resist talking about himself for a bit. I just needed the distraction and the time to wiggle my way out of these restraints. When I woke up and realized where I was, I felt around as much as possible and felt that the screws were loose on the table. I've slowly been undoing the screw with my fingernail as he's been going on and on about taking the time to tell his story or not.

The screws were just the right amount of loose for me to manage to continue twisting with just my fingernail. Hopefully, He'll tell a long enough story for me to finish it. All I would have to do at that point is wait for him to bring something over to the table so I can use it against him. Like I told him before, I know how to survive, and he thinks that he's the one that's going to win this. He already lost the moment he chose an old man to control.

So where would you like me to start?" He asked me, staring into my eyes. "I'll play along and let you ask the questions."

"Well, I suppose you could start with your parents." I responded.

"Let's see here." He began. "My father was an alcoholic and hardly around. One day he won big playing cards, and that was the last time I saw him. He most likely either drank himself to death or gambled the rest of it away and owed someone money and they must have taken care of him. Either way I haven't seen or heard from him after that night and didn't care to look for him either."

"What about your mother?" I asked, looking at his face.

"Now that's a whole other story there." He said as he leaned back, not looking thrilled at the question. "My mother, on the other hand, was a strong, independent woman. She had to be both mother and father to me. She was a religious woman that attended the local church and lived by a strict code. She would discipline me for everything that I did wrong or not do right in the eyes of her and God. She could be very mean at times, well, or most of the time. I had to follow her strict guidelines, but as a growing boy I used to break them all the time."

I watched him look away for a second, seeing his hands clenched at the thought of her and her behavior towards him. As I observed his behavior, I continued to work on the screws.

"My mother used all the tricks in the book to discipline my ass." He continued. "I would get a wooden ruler, or a paddle on my ass. I would get locked in a closet from time to time. I would go for a while without food or water. I would have to do the most disgusting chores possible. I was secluded away from society for a while. All I had to do was take care of the house and make mother happy and proud."

"Sounds like tough love to me." I said with an evil grin on my face.

"With the abandonment from my father and the strict ways from my mother, rage and anger flowed through my body at an exponential rate." He said, ignoring my last statement. "I battled with myself for a while on how to control my rage and anger. I didn't know what to take it out on. I was still young and couldn't win any fights, so I decided to take my anger out on animals."

"What did you end up doing to the animals?" I asked as I finally was able to get one of the screws undone.

"Oh, I ended up destroying all kinds of animals." He said with a smile across his face. "One time, we had a rat problem. My job was to find a way to get rid of them. Well, I didn't know many ways of doing so at the time. I ended up catching one. Instead of letting it go down the road, or killing it fast, I took my sweet time with it."

"What did you end up doing to it?" I asked, curious as to what happened.

"I slow-cooked it." He said, still smiling at me. "I put it into a pot with a lid and threw it on the stove. I had the flames on low because I wanted to watch them slowly die. After a bit on the stove, I turned the heat up and watched the animal go crazy in the pot. The rat crawled and scratched the sides of the pot. It was doing anything and everything to survive. Eventually the rat died and I took its body and tied it to a stick. Almost like throwing a body up on a cross, I threw the mouse's body onto a stick as well and planted it by where I believed the mouse came from. I wanted it to be a message to the other rats not to invade my space."

I shudder at the imagery. He's very sick. He did that at a young age. I don't even want to know what he did next to other animals, but I need more time. I almost have the other screw loose.

"I'm taking it you didn't stop with the rat?" I point out, rather than ask the question.

"Oh, no." He said with a smile. "That was just the beginning."

"What did you do next?" I was afraid to ask.

"I started setting up traps all through the yard. I was hoping to get different kinds of critters. I ended up catching squirrels, chipmunks, bunnies, and skunks. One time I managed to catch a coon. That coon was fat and plump. Some of the animals I let starve. I wanted to see how long they would go without food or water. I wanted to find out how long they could survive and what they would do to survive. I can't recall which animal did it, but one of them tried to chew through its own foot to escape."

He started to laugh at the thought of the animal eating itself as he closed his eyes, picturing the scene. It made me wonder if it would work on him too. What if I tied him up in a trap? Would he eventually try to chew his own foot to escape?

"Is that all you did?" I asked, not wanting to hear the answer. "Just catch the animals and observe them?"

"At first I did." He answered. Eventually my curiosity was getting the better of me. I started to wonder exactly how they moved. What was inside of them. I decided to take my studies even further. I researched the anatomy of the different animals. I memorized each bone and organ that was inside of the animals. The real fun began when I started to dissect the animals. I fully got the inside scoop of each kind, if you know what I mean."

As he finished the sentence, he let out an evil laugh. It's an image that I can't get out of my head. A young doctor, probably sitting in a garage or shed poking around and dismembering animals, justifying that it's for research purposes.

"And I'm taking it that's what led to humans?" I asked already, knowing the answer to the question.

"The interest in the animals sparked my interest in the human form. I realized how easy it was for me to memorize the bones and structures of these animals and figured it would be just as easy for me to memorize those in humans. I began my studies and became a doctor soon after. It didn't take long for me to find my first victim."

"Who was your first victim?" I asked curiously.

"My Mother was my first victim." He answered, observing my reactions. "I finally had the strength to give her a taste of her own medicine after the years of abuse she made me endure. I finally had my first test subject. I took her down into my basement and threw her onto a table. I marked her entire body so I could, firsthand, view her entire human system. From the muscular system down to the skeletal system. With each layer, I grew with excitement and anticipation. I loved every single moment and cherished every second. I got to spend my first time with my mother, so it was a family ordeal."

I watched him smile to himself. After each segment of his historical story, he ends up laughing at himself. Closing his eyes each time, savoring the memory. By this time, I was able to loosen the second screw. Now, all I have to do is use the screw and try to cut my way out of the restraints. I need a little bit more time. I hope he has more of his awful, stupid stories.

"By the time I was done with my mother, I wanted more subjects." He explained without me asking for more. "I had a need for more. I would go out and find someone to work on in between my classes at the university. I used people's bodies to excel in my studies and eventually graduated and became a doctor. I moved to a small town and became a town doctor, helping everyone with their pathetic needs. Once I became trusted in the town, it was easy for me to take the ones that wouldn't be missed and continue my work on them. Only this time it wasn't for research; it was for torture. The torture made me feel things that I have never felt before. I was never a sexually active male growing up, thanks to my mother, but the way the torture made me feel, it was like I was partaking in sexual relations."

I cringe at that last statement. Of course, the sick fuck gets off on the torture. I haven't seen or heard him taking advantage of a single woman, and he hasn't touched me in any way. I managed to cut through the first restraint. The screw end was very sharp, and to be honest, I did not see it working. All I need is one more restraint to cut through. I just need a little bit more time.

"That's enough of my story." He said as he finally got out of the chair. "All the talk about torture makes me want to fulfill my need."

He makes his way to the back of the room. I could hear him going through cabinets and shelves looking for something he could use on me.

"Oh, this is just fitting." He said with a laugh.

I can hear him heading back over to me. He set something down on the table next to me. It looked like a cage. I strained my neck as far as possible and realized he had a cage with a rat in it. He moved back towards the back of the room, looking for something else. After a moment of rummaging through stuff he made his way back over to me.

"Look at what I have here." He said, gleaming down at me. "This will be your new friend."

He took a knife and cut into my shirt, exposing my bare stomach. As he opened the cage to take out the rat, I watched in horror. With his other hand, he set the pot down on my stomach. He slid the rat under the pot and watched my eyes get bigger. I can feel the rat move around my bare stomach, running around in circles. The whiskers are tickling my skin. I tried my best to ignore the tickling feeling and tried to put all my concentration on cutting through the other restraint. I feel as if I'm getting closer to freeing my wrist.

"Let me tell you another story about the rat and the pot." He said, smiling at me, watching my eyes bulge.

Yes. Go ahead and tell me another story. I thought to myself. Give me that much-needed extra time to fully cut through this last restraint.

Chapter Thirty-Six: Julie

I still feel the little rat running in circles under the pot. The sharp tickling is starting to drive me crazy. It's such a weird feeling. Its tail and whiskers are tickling my skin, while its claws are scratching my bare skin. As I'm trying to block out the weird sensation, I watch Lou walk around and eventually turn his back on me. I'm still trying to furiously cut through the other restraint with the screw. I can feel it starting to give way.

"One last story for you, my dear." He said as he walked over by the blocked window. He has his hands held behind his back. "It's ironic for the rat since it was my first specimen I used to begin my research and training. It's funny that I just told you that story. The story I'm about to tell you is how that rat was used as a torture method."

I watched as he continued to pace back and forth by the window. He's not even paying attention to me. He probably figures that I'm secure and that I won't go anywhere. This little story he's about to tell me will give me just enough time to finally get through the last restraint.

"You see." He begins again. "The Russian Mafia used this method to get snitches to confess to them that they've been telling their secrets to those that shouldn't know their business. It seems like a harmless method, but it gets quite gruesome. The Mob would put a rat under a bucket or pot, like the one that's on you right now. The individual would be tied up, so they couldn't squirm away. You then apply heat to the outside of the bucket or pot and hold the heat to it. The hotter it becomes, the more the rat will try to run away. Now, the rat can't escape from under the bucket or pot, so where will it go? When there's too much heat for the rat to bare?"

He looks over at me for a moment, expecting me to give him an answer, but then he turns away, no longer waiting for a response from me.

"The only way for the rat to escape is down. It will scratch and chew its way through the individual's stomach to escape. And trust me, that rat will end up surviving. The individual, on the other hand, won't survive the punishment."

"Well, where's the satisfaction in the torture if the rat just ends up killing the person?" I asked, trying to see where his mind was at.

"That's the thing." He said, looking over to me. "You must know when to stop applying the heat. You only want the rat to scratch and chew to a certain limit. The Mob would go in sessions depending on if the individual still had more information they needed. If the individual had no longer use, they would just let the rat do its thing to survive the heat."

I watched as he headed towards the back of the room. I can hear him digging around for something else. As he's searching for God knows what else, I finally cut through the other restraint. Both of my hands are now free, but I made it look like I was still tied down. He came back to me holding a torch in his hand. Makes sense; that's what he was looking for. Unfortunately for him, he's not going to be able to use it.

He turned his head for a moment, giving me precisely the right amount of time to grab the pot and hit him over the head with it. I struck him fast and hard, seeing him hit the floor quickly. Lou is an old man; it wouldn't take much to knock his ass out. The doctor should have picked a better candidate to come after me.

I looked down and noticed a small pool of blood coming from the gash on the head where I struck him with the pot. I could see his body move up and down slightly, so I knew he was still breathing, but he was not moving a muscle.

I bent over and started to unfasten the restraints on my ankles. As soon as I got the restraints off, I jumped off and checked on Lou. He was still breathing, but out cold. My plan worked. That goes to show no one fucks with me. I've had enough today. I looked around the floor to see if I could spot the rat, but it ran off too. Good for him. I also saved a rat's life. At least I did some kind of good today.

I reached down and grabbed Lou's body. This man was very light, even with his dead weight. I placed him up on the table and grabbed some new rope. I double-bound his limbs to the table to make sure there was no way for him to escape.

Satisfied with myself, I searched for the smelling salts. Time to wake his ass up.

Chapter Thirty-Seven: Julie

I popped the smelling salts under his nose and watched him take a deep breath. He blinked his eyes open and looked around almost in a frantic way. He looked to his left, then to his right, and I could tell that he was trying to wiggle his wrists free.

"Goddamnit." He let out a shout with a wince from his head injury.

"What was it you were saying about winning?" I asked him, smiling down at him.

"You fucking bitch!" He cried at me.

It was my turn to laugh at him. He's all tied up and it looks funny. Seeing the old man useless and bonded to the table. Instantly I felt this sudden urge of power and excitement. I also feel like a bunch of weight is lifted off my shoulders.

"What's wrong doc?" I asked, still having a huge ass smile on my face.

"There's no way you could have escaped!" He continues to shout.

"I twisted off the loose screws on the table." Looking down at my bloody fingernails. Tired and in pain from the amount of work it took to cut free. "Then I used those screws to cut through the restraints."

"Not possible!" He said, staring at me.

"What is it you say?" I asked him. "If there's a will, there's a   way?"

"What are you going to end up doing?" He asks, puzzled. "Where you going to end up when this is all over?"

"Well, I could call the cops right now." I began to explain. "But I can't be certain that they can take my side in this. Especially after everything that I've done. Also, who said I'll even return home?"

"I knew I wasted too much time." He speaks. "I should have just begun the torture right away!"

"A bit too late for that!" I protested. "Don't you think?"

I went to the back of the room searching for something. Where is it? I asked myself. It's got to be here somewhere. I scanned the wall, and then the surrounding table. I still couldn't find what I was looking for until I saw a bag on the floor with a handle sticking out of it. There it is. I went over to the bag and opened it up. I reached into the bag to pull it out.

I held the shaft in my hands and peered at it. The blade of the hatchet was still extremely sharp.

I headed back to the table and held the hatchet up for Lou to see. I slowly rubbed my fingers over the blade. I can feel the cool, sharp edge as I run across its length. I looked over at the table next to me and saw that the torch was still sitting on the table. There's only one more tool missing. I remember seeing it resting on the back table. I returned to the back table to retrieve it. It's a rounded tool to cauterize the limbs after amputation.

"Time for your own medicine." I said, gleaming down at him.

I raised the hatchet in his left hand and struck down hard and fast. I severed his hand at the wrist. Blood gushing and squirting out from the missing limb. I quickly heated up the tool, and once it got nice and hot, I cauterized the wound shut.

"One down." I said, enjoying myself. "Three more to go."

I wasted no time. I raised the hatchet once again and severed his right hand. The tool didn't take as long to heat up this time as I brought it down to cauterize the wound. The smell of burning flesh filled the air surrounding us. The smell was horrid. I gagged a few times as the smell filled my nostrils. I don't know how anyone could be able to do this.

I looked at Lou's face. It's a ghostly color. I'm not sure how much more punishment he could stand. He's a weak old man. I'm surprised he's lasted with these two amputations. Sweat poured down his face. He closed his eyes a few times tightly. He hasn't spoken a word in a bit. Suddenly, he lets out a laugh. What the fuck? He's laughing right now. How does he have the energy and strength to let out a laugh and not a cry to make it stop? It must be the strength of the mind of the doctor. It's the only way.

Fine. I raised the hatchet above his left ankle and came down fast and hard. His ankle was severed in a matter of seconds. More blood is added to the collection under the table. I applied heat to the circular tool once more and cauterized the wound.

Lou is looking worse by the second, but he continues to laugh. The doctor's mind is stronger than I expected. He just lays there on the table looking at the missing body parts and laughs menacingly.

"Only one more left." I say, looking at his pale face. "What the fuck is wrong with you? Why are you laughing?"

"You think I feel pain?" He asks me. "His mind is mine to control. I'm blocking out the pain receptors."

"That must take most of your energy to do so." I state. "I can see physically the amount of pain you have to block out."

Out of rage and anger, I raised the hatchet one last time and struck down, severing the other ankle. I decided against cauterizing this limb. Maybe with the bleeding out it'll take him more energy to block out the pain. This should keep him from following me.

"You can't block out the pain forever." I said, watching the weak old man show the amount of pain he'd endured.

"Are you not going to finish?" He asked me.

"What do you mean?" I responded.

"You're forgetting the final step." He said through shortened breaths and gritted teeth.

"Oh, the head." I laugh. "No, I'm not going to cut the head off. I'm going to let you bleed out. Eventually you'll feel the pain, and you won't have the ability to come after me. I'll be long gone.

"Again." He began, looking at me through pain-filled eyes. "For as clever as you are, you are quite dumb."

"Sure." I responded.

"Don't worry." He looks at me, still giving off a laugh. "I have a new plan for you."

I didn't respond to him this time. Whatever that last comment meant, I shrugged it off and walked away from the table. I took the hatchet in my hand, and without another look, I walked out of the boathouse. I'm going to take his truck and leave this place for good.

Chapter Thirty-Eight: Doctor Jacob Underwood

Oh, this bitch is dumber than I thought. In her head she thinks she's won. That she has the upper hand. She forgot one thing. One important aspect of all this. She let her rage and emotion get the best of her. The best thing about survival is making sure you have all the means to survive. She will soon find out that she didn't prepare herself well enough.

I floated above Lou's body and looked at his missing limbs. I'll tell you what, though: this girl has gall. She can be useful. Unfortunately, using Lou worked only to get to her. I should have used someone more physically for the torture part. I was in too much of a hurry. That was my fault. My weakness. The good part about all this is it has led me to a whole new level of doing things.

I will never go away. I will never quit. I will never let someone escape my clutches. I've told her this once. I always find a way to win. As I made my way outside, I watched Julie step inside Lou's truck.

That's right darling, make your escape. I will let you think that you are free for a bit. You won't even know what will hit you next.

Chapter Thirty-Nine: Julie

I climbed inside Lou's truck. I placed the hatchet down on the passenger-side seat. Blood was still coming off the blade. Probably not the best place to put it, but I don't give a shit. I just want out of here.

I started the truck and turned around to head down the trail to the main road. Once I got to the intersection, I paused for a moment. If I turn left, I'll head back home, but if I turn right, I'll be off in a new direction.

After a moment. I didn't hesitate. I turned right. I've made up my mind. I'll go somewhere new. Start over. A new beginning. I'll change my appearance. I'll find a job that doesn't require me to have a degree. I could survive that way.

Maybe I could live on a farm or something. Take care of animals and livestock. Not that I know how to do any of that. Or maybe I can find a wealthy male to share his money with. I'll just provide him with children and tend to household duties. I'll keep everything I've been through a secret.

As I continued down the road, I started to feel kind of funny. I felt different. I can't really explain the feeling I'm having. My head hurts and my vision is slightly blurry. Maybe I'm getting a massive migraine. This could be a possibility, with the amount of stress and lack of sleep I've been under lately.

"Or maybe you could just live out in the middle of nowhere and kill for me." A voice said in my mind.

What the fuck was that? I swerved the truck at the random voice that I heard. I went over to the side of the road and stopped the truck. When the truck came to a stop, I looked around. I looked to my right and left, then looked in the back seat; no one was around. Then I heard it again.

"You thought you were going to win?" The voice continued.

I looked in the rearview mirror and rubbed my face. What the fuck is happening?

"Who's there? I asked, still looking around at my surroundings.

"Isn't it obvious who's there?" The voice said once more.

"This can't be happening!" I cried out. I must be extremely tired.

"You're not tired. This is happening. You are hearing me just fine."

"What you want from me?" I asked, looking dumb, my eyes darting all over the place.

"I made it very clear that you won't win." The voice said to me. *"I will always win!"*

"No, this can't be real!" I cried out. "I left you on the table!"

"I also told you that you were clever but not very smart." The voice said. *"You forgot one important detail in your final stand against me."*

"What?" I cried out. "What did I forget?"

"Just like I left your boyfriend." The voice began to explain. *"I left Lou's mind. Now here I am. You've given me another idea. I wanted to torture you to death, but you've proven useful to me."*

"No!" I started to cry out. "Stay away from me!"

"I'm afraid it's too late, my dear."

Suddenly, the pain in my head grew more intense. I grabbed a hold of my head and closed my eyes. When I opened my eyes, everything began to spin. I felt like I was going to vomit from the spinning and the pain. My vision went blank.

I opened my eyes and looked in the rearview mirror. The reflection that glared back was that of a salt-n-pepper-headed man. Julie was no longer in the reflection. The strength and power that I felt was amazing. I looked down at the passenger-side seat and picked up the hatchet. I looked through the mirror one last time, seeing my handsome self with the hatchet right in front of my face. I gave off a huge smile.

"We have work to do, Julie."

End